HERE WITH YOU FOREVER

BRIANN DANAE

MESSAGE

Gentle reminder... just because *you* wouldn't doesn't mean someone else can't. Also, this is fiction. Enjoy, and happy reading!

FORBIDDEN
ETERNALLY
UNWAVERING

LET'S STAY IN TOUCH

Instagram

instagram.com/brianndanae

TikTok

www.tiktok.com/@brianndanae

Facebook

www.facebook.com/brianndanae

Mailing List

https://bit.ly/BDWSubscribe

TRIGGER WARNINGS

-Heavy mentions of grief

PLAYLIST

If you're a music lover like me, enjoy the playlist I created to feel all the vibes while reading or after you're done. Scan the code, add it to your library, and enjoy!

Apple Music

Spotify Music

"FAMILY WILL BE THE FIRST TO HURT YOU."

ONE

"Your daddy said, why aren't you answering the phone?"

Leerah knew she should've ignored her mama's call, but knowing Katrina Canady, she'd only send a text message telling her only daughter to call her back. She hadn't been off work a good ten minutes, and the questions, though appreciated, had already begun.

"He knows what time I clock out of work, Mama," Leerah answered. "It's been the same time for the past two years."

"Well, he obviously needs a reminder." Katrina chuckled. "And don't be that way. You know he just wants to hear your voice. See how you're doing."

These days, that seemed to be the only thing

people wanted to know about Leerah; how she was doing, how she was feeling, what type of mood she was in, and other questions she'd respond to with "I'm fine." The questions were open-ended, allowing her to share as little as possible.

Her answer was far from the truth.

Explaining how she really felt wasn't a conversation Leerah was ready to have with her mama, especially after her good workday. It'd put her in a crappy mood, and she didn't want that.

"I'll call him back once I get home," Leerah said.

"You and my grandbaby should come over for dinner."

Her mama's suggestion didn't sound too bad; plus, that'd be one less task she'd have to worry about for the evening. She didn't give it any thought before agreeing.

"We should. What you cooking?" Leerah questioned, knowing it really didn't matter. Whatever it was, beat takeout or what she'd have to pull out of the freezer.

"Chicken tetrazzini and some cornbread with a Caesar salad," Katrina answered.

Leerah licked her lips. "That sounds too good. You know I love me a salad."

They chuckled, knowing that was nothing but

the truth. It didn't matter what restaurant they went to; if there was salad on the menu, Leerah was ordering one.

"That I do," Katrina agreed.

"I'm headed to pick Landon up now, and we'll be there."

Katrina told her okay, and they hung up. There were days when no one could get Leerah to answer the phone. Staying to herself wasn't done purposefully, but some mornings, she woke up and didn't want to be bothered by anyone except her son. While most of her friends and family understood that, some didn't, and she quickly let them know that it was nothing personal.

When life unexpectedly forces you to grieve, sometimes you have to isolate yourself or you'll lose your mind.

Being forced into being a single parent wasn't in the deck of cards Leerah shuffled and laid out, but... life. It showed you that not every hand was a good one, and you played what you were dealt. Leerah wanted to toss her deck in the trash and grab another. Surely, there had to be some favor in a new stack.

With the daycare close to her job, she made it to Little Learners in under twenty minutes. Leerah parked near the entrance, climbed out, and was buzzed in after being verified through the security camera. Serene tunes, kids' laughter, and cries, plus the sounds of Gracie's Corner in the distance, greeted her before Kenia, one of the staff, did. She was one of Terrance's first cousins on his mama's side and messy as hell. Her smirk let Leerah know she was ready to run her mouth about someone else.

"Hey, Leerah girl," Kenia greeted, waving her hand.

Leerah shook her head. "What's up, girl? They got you working the front this week?"

"No, just for today," she answered while Leerah signed Landon out on the iPad. "You not gon' believe who came in here this morning."

"Here you go, being messy."

Kenia laughed. "Telling you pertinent information I think you should know is not being messy."

"Is it going to change my life in any way?" Leerah asked.

"Nope, but who cares? Makai dropped some girl's child off this morning like he was daddy of the year. Talking about his girl was going to be late to work, so he brought little man in. Ain't he like twenty-two?"

"He's more of your family than he is mine, girl. I don't know," Leerah replied.

Compared to Leerah's two older brothers, her baby daddy, Terrance, had a gang of siblings. The Undisputed Truth was singing about Vince when they made *Papa Was a Rollin' Stone*. Though Kenia was kin through Andrea, Terrance's mama, anyone related to Terrance was considered family. So, seeing her younger cousin handling responsibilities like a grown man surprised her, and she wanted the tea. That was too bad because Leerah had none to share.

"True. But that's so crazy. I heard that girl's baby daddy is in jail, and here Makai comes wanting to step up. I guess."

Leerah couldn't hide her frown. "That's a problem?"

"Yeah, especially if he's about to get out. Makai better be careful. You know how men be about their seed."

"Right," Leerah mumbled. "That's his business, though."

"Thought I'd just let you know since Landon be around him."

Leerah wasn't trying to hear all that. If and when Makai was around his nephew, nine times out of ten, it was when Zola, Terrance's older brother's mama had him. What that man had going on was none of her concern.

"Girl, whatever. Go get my baby so I can get out of here."

Picking up the walkie-talkie, Kenia chirped one of the staff in the back, letting them know Landon was ready for pickup. While she waited, Leerah scrolled through her unread text messages.

"Oh. I meant to ask if we were invited to the birthday party," Kenia said.

Leerah gave her a deadpan stare. "Why would I not invite y'all? Don't piss me off."

"Don't say it like that. I just had to make sure. You know you be in your moods, ready to cut folks off."

"And do," Leerah said unapologetically.

It was no secret that people had lots to say about her once Terrance passed, especially his auntie and Kenia's mama, Vee, who also worked at the daycare. Leerah wasn't a secretive person; she just didn't like people in her business. Their opinions about a situation that had nothing to do with them always rubbed her the wrong way.

So, yes, she sometimes got in certain moods when it came to certain people because they tried playing in her face. Vee had so much to say when

Leerah popped up pregnant and voiced her concerns about the baby not being his. Terrance shut all that shit down and promised to stop speaking to her if she kept getting out of line. So, when he passed, and everyone found out that they weren't together, Vee felt like she had a one-up. But she didn't at all.

Leerah knew what her issue was and honestly couldn't have cared less. Misha, Terrance's first baby mama, and Vee were really close. Considering that was her nephew's first child, Leerah understood it, but Vee got beside herself some days, thinking Leerah wouldn't check her, either. She was sadly mistaken.

Speaking of Vee, she held Landon's hand as they walked to the front. Spotting his mommy, Landon took off running in her direction. Leerah couldn't help but laugh at his bow-legged run. He started walking at ten months old, and since finding his balance, he thought he could run everywhere.

"Hi, Mommy's baby," Leerah cooed, swooping him into her arms.

Nuzzling her face in the crook of his neck, she hugged him tightly before kissing his puffy cheeks. He took after Leerah with those while inheriting most of Terrance's other features. Considering how handsome Terrance had been, she didn't mind that at all. His light caramel complexion, soft curls, and bowlegs all came from him.

The myth was that if the baby came out looking just like the daddy, that meant the mama couldn't stand him for the majority of her pregnancy. To an extent, Leerah gave whoever made that up some credit. About half of her pregnancy wasn't spent the way she mapped it out in her mind, but delivering her happy little baby was all that mattered.

"He's getting so big," Kenia acknowledged, grinning.

Landon smiled big as Leerah adjusted him on her hip. "Right. I can't believe he's about to be one."

"And hello to you too, missy," Vee greeted.

Leerah eyed her before dryly saying, "Hey." Vee's faux smile wasn't getting her.

Vee shook her head. "Is it always going to be like this when we see one another?"

"Like what, Ms. Vee?" Leerah questioned, wanting her to say what it really was instead of beating around the bush.

Leerah would've done the honors but was trying to remember her manners.

"Like you have a problem with me."

Leerah sighed. "I don't have an issue with you,

and here lately, you've been keeping your shady remarks to yourself. So, I would hope we were all good considering my son goes here."

Vee scrunched her face up. "We're family. I would never in my life bring harm to Landon. I surely hope you don't think that."

"That's good to know because I don't play about my son. Family will be the first to hurt you, but okay. I hear you," Leerah said.

"Well, you don't have to worry about that or the payment this week."

"Why not?" Leerah wondered.

Vee stepped closer to her just as another parent entered the building. Leerah scooted off to the side, slightly nervous about what she could've possibly been about to tell her.

"So, I've been hearing some things," Vee started.

Good to know you can hear, Leerah thought. "Things about what?"

"Just a certain someone who shouldn't be taking a liking to you considering you all's relationship."

Leerah huffed in annoyance. "The likes of me? You're talking in circles. Just tell me what's going on so I can head out."

"Is there a reason why Cree covered your fees for the next three months?" Vee questioned.

Leerah tried her best to hide her disgust and shock at her question, but she knew she had failed when Vee's eyes widened.

"The same reason why your sister, Terrance's mama, filled my fridge and cabinets up with groceries last week. Because she wanted to. I can't even believe you're standing here questioning me about some shit like that!" Leerah spat. "Of all things, you're worried about Cree, who, to my knowledge, is something like your nephew, providing for Landon? Is you coo'?"

Vee blinked rapidly, somewhat taken aback by Leerah's harsh tone. "I just found it odd."

"No, you found yourself jealous yet again, and for what? I have no idea. Probably because you've been sitting up gossiping about something you have no clue about. Let me tell you something, Ms. Vee, and I hope I never have to repeat myself again. I'm Landon's mama. Terrance, your nephew, died okay? He's not coming back. My baby doesn't have a fucking father in his life, so you know where most of the responsibility of caring for our child lands... on me. Thankfully, I have a community of people who don't mind taking some of the weight off, but it's envious people like you who can't fathom that they would ever. News flash: they will and always have had my back. If you have a problem with that, that's too damn bad."

"I've been trying to keep it real cordial with you for the sake of my son, but you're trying it. Don't worry about how things are being handled in my household. If a man wants to pay all my bills for as long as I live, I'ma let him, and that is none of your business. Maybe if you had a man, you wouldn't feel so entitled or have time to speak on anyone else's life. Now, excuse me," Leerah said, brushing by her. "I need to get going."

Vee grabbed her arm, and you would've thought Leerah burned her with her eyes the way she snatched it away. She didn't even have to tell her not to touch her.

"All I'm saying is that Landon is ours just as much as he is yours, and I don't want there to be any confusion. No man is doing that unless—"

"Unless they care about someone. That someone happens to be Landon, whom I pushed out of my pussy. The only person who's confused by that is you."

Before she smacked her and called her a hating ass bitch who needed to rotate and balance her wig like some tires and adjust her too-small bra, Leerah exited the building.

"See y'all later!" Kenia shouted after them.

Beyond annoyed with what had just gone down, Leerah yanked the back door open and tossed Landon's bag inside. When he looked her upside the head like she was crazy, Leerah couldn't help but chuckle.

"I'm sorry, stinka butt. Your bag didn't do anything to me," she said, kissing his cheek.

After buckling him in, Leerah climbed in the driver's seat and peeled out of the parking lot. Vee had her fucked up on so many levels. Leerah had the right mind to call and tell her mama. Katrina raised her not to disrespect her elders, but she got down with the best of them and would check Vee's hateful ass quick behind her child and grandbaby.

"That lady really tried me," Leerah fumed, tightening her hands around the steering wheel.

Had she not had Landon with her, Leerah would've talked worse to her; give her a rundown on the shit she'd heard about her since everyone's "business" was getting aired out. It was so disheartening witnessing the level of hate in someone's eyes for her, and Leerah couldn't understand why. She'd be lying if she said it didn't bother her because it did.

Granted she hadn't been around Terrance's family for long, almost four years now, but time shouldn't have mattered. It was a respect thing, and Vee had none for her. She'd made that abundantly clear more than once, and Leerah was done holding her tongue and being nice about anything concerning her moving forward. Terrance was the only reason she even allowed Landon to go to the daycare, but now that was about to come to an end.

You'd think having someone cover her bill would've been considered a good thing, but of course, Vee had to make it something it wasn't. One thing Leerah hadn't had to do or had never done was ask for a handout. If and when people wanted to provide for her, it happened because they did it on their own. If anything, especially regarding Landon, needed to be handled, she was figuring it out. Terrance not being here wasn't stopping a thing.

However, his absence offered a loneliness that Leerah wasn't fond of. They weren't in a relationship when he passed away, but they were still friends. At least, that's what Leerah had tried convincing him that was the only thing they were. Terrance wasn't trying to co-parent, but he also wasn't trying to be faithful. Leerah knew this.

They broke up when Landon was two months old, but Terrance never once half-stepped when it came to his fatherly duties. If a diaper needed to be changed, clothes needed to be washed, the house needed to be cleaned, doctor's appointments needed to be made, and much more, he was there. Leerah applauded him for being a great father, but he lacked as a boyfriend.

With a child now in the picture, the last thing Leerah was worried about was trying to make it work with a man who obviously had other plans. As she drove to her parents' house, Leerah couldn't help but think back to the few days before his death. She'd never been the one to mince her words, but had she known that would've been their last encounter, Leerah would've held back some.

Months Ago

L*eerah's eyes were glued to the TV, and Terrance's were glued to her. He'd bathed Landon, and right after that, Leerah breastfed him until he fell asleep. She had him on a strict bedtime schedule, and they were usually knocked out and in bed by nine o'clock. Had Leerah's show not come on, she would've been knocked out right beside him. Terrance finally said something when she yawned during the last couple minutes of her show.*

"You really on some bullshit, Leerah."

"Dang. I can't yawn?"

He glared at her from the other end of the sectional and shook his head. "You know what I'm talking about, man. What are we doing?"

With a quick commercial break, Leerah gave him her undivided attention. When he asked what they were doing and wanted to have serious conversations with her, Leerah knew she had to stay strong and not fold under the scrutiny of his hazel eyes. Terrance was the dangerous type of fine with long locs, juicy pinkish brown lips, stood at six feet one, could make you laugh, and applied straight pressure when it came to her. That was how he grabbed and kept her attention when they first met.

Leerah had just arrived at a day party on Vine, annoyed with one of the men doing security at the door and had the meanest mug on her face. Terrance was posted up with his homeboys peeping the scene, and she immediately captured his attention. After learning who she was, he approached her and asked how he could make her day better so she'd stop frowning. Leerah snapped on him, telling him to get out of her face, and that only made him press her more. They exchanged numbers and had been in one another's lives since then.

"I'm doing me, and you're doing you," Leerah replied, shrugging.

Terrance gritted his teeth. "The fuck does that mean?"

"It means that nothing is changing between us because you want it to. When I wanted to make things work between us and have a family, you were on bull-shit, so stay on that. I'm coo'."

He scanned her face for evidence of a lie, trying to call her bluff. "I told you I cut them hoes off. You still trippin' about old shit."

Leerah rolled her eyes. "Your words don't mean much to me anymore. Especially not when I can see things for what it really is. No need to try and keep playing house when you don't even come home to it." She laughed, further pissing him off.

"That's what you were getting. Me coming home to you and my son, and then you switched up."

"You mean I switched up after you were out embar-rassing me? Do I look like a goofy bitch to you?" Leerah cocked her head to the left, amusement dancing in her eyes. "You came home to us after having your fun and expected me to just sit back and be okay with that, and I never will be. If the streets are what you want, baby, go play in them. Just don't expect me to be waiting around when you're done."

Terrance's nostrils flared as Leerah's attention went back to the TV. She was calm and assertive. She always had been, but he noticed that she wasn't trying to argue with him. The Leerah he met years ago would've been shouting in his face about playing with her and cursing him out. She wasn't that girl anymore but now a woman who knew her worth. Having a child and becoming a mother had matured her, and Leerah wasn't putting up with any more of his bullshit.

"So, we over just like that, huh?" Terrance questioned, scooting to the edge of the couch.

Leerah glanced his way. "We been over, so what's up? Why are you looking all upset? No one told you to do the things you do and move how you did, Terrance. If you wanted to be a family and make shit work between us, you would've done that."

"You ain't even give a nigga time to get it right."

She chuckled. "Baby, time has been on your side, and now it's up. I don't know what else you want me to tell you."

"Damn." Terrance scoffed. "All that love you claim you had for a nigga just gon' like that. Poof!" he said, dramatically demonstrating with his hands.

Leerah held back her laugh. "Love and tolerating disrespect are two different things, and I'm not accepting both, so..." she said and shrugged. "What if I were out here all in men's faces, acting like I didn't have a man or child at home?"

"You ain't even that type of girl, and you know I ain't going for none of that shit," Terrance snarled.

Leerah smirked. "Nope, I'm not that kind of girl, but I can be."

"Man, quit fucking playin' with me 'fore I snatch that wig off your head."

When he stood up and walked over to the couch, Leerah laughed while tossing pillows at him. Playfully, Terrance held her down and smothered her with kisses. She squirmed with laughter while pushing him off of her. Hovering above her, Terrance stared her in the eyes. The love still resided in them, but he saw hurt as well. He'd fucked up a good thing but would do whatever to get it back. When he leaned in for a kiss, Leerah dodged it, pushing against his chest.

"Un, un. Ain't no more fucking and making up," she protested.

"How 'bout we just fuck then? I know you miss this dick."

Leerah hated how her body still responded to him. Her heart, though... it didn't crave him like it did before. Consistently being disappointed by Terrance when she used to have so much faith in him dwindled her heart's yearning for him.

She shook her head. "Nope. Plus, that phone in your pocket vibrating almost made me slap you. So, watch it."

She shoved him harder and stood from the couch. Terrance could ignore the girl calling his phone all he wanted to, but Leerah wasn't. When she walked past him, trying to head to the kitchen, Terrance caught her around the waist and hugged her from behind. The smell of his cologne, and the feel of his soft beard and locs against her face almost made her cave.

"You so mean now. I turned you into this person?" he questioned softly, wanting to know the truth.

Leerah swallowed her tears down. She didn't want to admit that and seem weak, so she shook her head no.

"No, you turned me into the woman I should've been long before now."

Her answer gutted Terrance. His actions caused Leerah to gain some clarity and realize that just because they shared a child didn't mean they had to be together. Every fuck up he made, made Leerah reconsider the type of life she wanted for not just her but Landon as well. The decisions she made from here on out affected them both.

Trying to make things work only on one end was frustrating, so she let it go. It would hurt—it did hurt— but mentally, she had to do what was best for her. Terrance hugged her tighter, resting his head against her shoulder.

"Man, you make that sound so fucked up, like I just

dogged you. You know I love the fuck outta you," Terrance professed.

"Mhm. I love you too, homeboy, but I love me more."

"Homeboy?" Terrance sneered. "Keep playing."

Leerah giggled. "That's what you are."

"Yeah, a'ight. What about Landon?"

Leerah angled her head. "What about him?"

"You ain't gon' be on no petty, spiteful shit and not let me get him, are you? I ain't no part-time ass daddy."

She chuckled. "Boy, I know that, but no. I would never keep him from you. You should know me better than that."

"Nah. I knew the old you. This new Leerah done fucked my head up, but I guess that's on me, huh?"

She sighed, wishing things didn't have to be this way. "I guess so."

Terrance kissed her cheek and released her from his hold. She turned to face him. "It's all good, though. I'ma get back on my shit and come back for what's mine. Y'all my family regardless of what we going through."

Leerah laughed. "Yeah, unless another nigga come snatch us up."

"There you go, talking stupid," he said, reaching out to mush her in the head.

She swatted his arm away. "Move. You better gon' head before whoever calling you gets upset."

"I ain't tripping. Give me a kiss, and I'll leave." Terrance smiled, showing off his perfect smile with a slight gap.

Before she could deny him again, he pressed his lips against hers and spanked her on the ass. Disgusted, Leerah wiped her mouth with the back of her hand.

"Ugh. I don't know where your mouth has been," she fussed.

"It could be on you, but you faking like that shit ain't mine," Terrance smirked, grabbing his keys off the table. "I'll be through here to get my son tomorrow."

She playfully rolled her eyes. "He's our son and okay. Just call me."

Leerah followed him to the door and stopped walking when Terrance did. He looked back at her, and Leerah's brows dented, waiting to hear what else he had to say.

"I'ma get my shit together, a'ight?"

His reiteration of what he was going to do didn't make Leerah believe him more or any less. She wanted Terrance to get his shit together for himself, not because there was a future for them as a couple. Only time would tell if his actions matched his words.

"I can't wait to see it," she said.

Terrance stared at her for a few seconds more before pulling the door open and walking out. When she locked it behind him, Leerah let out a heavy sigh. She hoped *that tonight they had come to some common ground of understanding.*

As promised, Terrance picked Landon up the next day. Instead of meeting her at the crib, he swung by the daycare and grabbed him. It was Friday, and the only plans Leerah had were to relax and clean up her apartment. Terrance called her on FaceTime once she was at home so she could talk to Landon, and the remainder of her night consisted of chilling.

Saturday morning rolled around, and Leerah was up early, tackling every room in the house while R&B jams played on the TV. She ran a few errands and linked up with one of her friends, Nae, for a bite to eat before heading back inside. By midnight, she was waking up from a nap and watching a movie series on Apple TV. When her phone vibrated with an incoming call two hours later, Leerah frowned.

"Who's calling me this late," she mumbled, reading over the unknown number.

She didn't answer but felt obligated to when the caller dialed her right back.

"Hello?" she questioned, voice laced with suspicion while placing the call on speaker.

"Aye, Leerah. This Cree. I'm glad you picked up."

She adjusted in bed, wondering why he was calling

her so late and from a number she didn't have his name saved under.

"What's up?" she questioned.

"It's Terrance," Cree started and cleared his throat. "He was in a car accident, and it's not looking too good."

"What! What do you mean it's not looking too good? Where is he?"

Leerah hopped out of bed, tripping over her comforter. While Cree ran down the details of what hospital they were headed to, she stripped from her pajamas, tossed on a bra, and hurriedly slid into some leggings and a t-shirt. She slid into a pair of sandals and rushed out of the house, almost forgetting to grab her purse or lock the door.

Purposefully taking back streets to avoid Saturday night traffic, Leerah's hands trembled the entire drive to the hospital. The only other time she could recall praying as hard as she had on the drive there, was when she was in labor.

"Lord, please let him be okay," she said aloud, pulling into the hospital's emergency entrance.

Spotting a few familiar faces rushing inside, Leerah's stomach churned as she parked. When she rushed inside, the deafening sound of someone screaming 'no' halted her steps. Looking ahead, she spotted Terrance's mama being held by her husband as she broke down. Wails from the other friends and family dazed Leerah. Her body was frozen in time as tears filled her eyes. Everything and everyone around her went radio silent.

No. This can't be happening, she thought to herself.

It wasn't until Cree came over and touched her arm that she regained her sense of hearing. With a heaving chest and trembling lips, she looked up at his saddened face.

"Cree... please. Is he...?"

She couldn't say the words. Wouldn't dare mumble them. All Cree could do was sadly nod, and Leerah crumbled into his embrace and broke down crying. Her screams came from the depths of her gut, but that didn't stop him from embracing her.

"I got you. I got you," Cree promised.

According to witnesses, a drunk driver had run a red light on 71 South, making Terrance's car flip. He had another person with him who was in critical condition while he stopped breathing on the ambulance ride over. Leerah couldn't wrap her mind around him no longer being here. She'd just spoken to him yesterday; now, he was gone.

Losing Terrance was still a hard pill to swallow, but the even tougher pill to get down was knowing that one day, she was going to have to explain to their son why he was no longer here. That hurt her beyond any pain Terrance could've ever caused her.

2
———

"THE MAN I AM ISN'T LETTING YOU DO THIS
ALONE."

TWO

"Leerah!"

Her head swiveled from where she was standing to locate her mama. Walking across the gymnasium, Leerah met her at the gift table that was already full.

"What's up, Mama?"

"We're going to need another table so people can sit down and eat. Go tell your brother to bring down another table," Katrina said.

Leerah underestimated the number of people who showed up and were still spilling in for Landon's first birthday party. When she sent out invitations via text message, many of them hadn't RSVP'd but were in attendance. She'd been finalizing things all week, ensuring her baby had the best day. Had it not been for her best friend, Sovanna, Nae, and her mama, Leerah wouldn't know what she would've done. Her emotions had been all over the place leading up to this day, and she'd already cried once.

Her eyes roamed the place for her oldest brother, Keith. Her second oldest brother, Marcus, was running late and hadn't arrived yet. Spotting him by the candy bags, Leerah walked over to him. She couldn't help but grin at the resemblance between him and their father. Making him his junior was perfect.

"I know you aren't over here stealing the candy?" Leerah joked.

Keith smirked. "Nah. Not yet. Everything good?"

"Yes, but Mama said grab another table so people can have somewhere to eat."

Scanning the crowd of people, Keith hoped he could spot the owner of the community center, Impact. Right on time, Krypt walked over. Leerah couldn't help but admire how fine he was. She didn't ogle for long out of respect for his wife, who was equally beautiful, along with their gorgeous son. She'd been in contact with them leading up to the party, and they had been nothing but helpful.

"Y'all need anything else?" Krypt asked, seeing the look on their faces.

"Yeah. A couple more tables and some chairs if y'all got them," Keith said.

Krypt nodded. "Yeah. Let me have a few of the staff bring some down."

"I'll follow you," Keith added.

"You good, Leerah?"

She nodded. "Yes. A few people have asked me about the swimming pool, and I told them we didn't rent that part out, so I'll make sure no one goes back there."

"The door is locked, but I 'preciate that. They can come through tomorrow when the lifeguards are on duty," Krypt said.

Impact was a newer community center in the heart of the city, and Krypt made sure to implement almost everything inside it that he didn't have growing up, as far as the rec center, he went to growing up. While they went to grab more tables and chairs, Leerah searched for Landon. He hadn't been placed down or left alone since he entered the building.

Seeing him at one of the bounce houses, she walked over and slipped her shoes off. They wore similar outfits. Leerah had on black acid-washed cargo pants with a white bootleg shirt displaying pictures of Landon on the front. His birthday outfit had been picked out months before things were even planned. Terrance wanted him in a Givenchy polo shirt, black jeans, and some white Forces. So, Leerah made it happen thanks to the help of his uncles.

"You having fun, baby?" Leerah smiled, watching him reach for her.

Picking him up, she climbed inside the bounce house and hopped around for a few before putting him down. With the other kids inside, Landon didn't stand a chance of keeping his balance, but that didn't stop him from hopping right back up. He laughed his little head off every time he fell over. Leerah pulled her phone out to capture the moment before getting tackled by one of her little cousins.

"Bryan! I'ma whoop your butt!" she hollered, laughing.

"You can't be in here on your phone! Those are the rules," he replied, laughing as he bounced away from her.

Leerah said forget the rules and climbed out. Landon was right behind her, not wanting to let her out of his sight. After slipping her shoes back on, she walked over to Sovanna, rubbing her baby hairs to make sure they were still in place.

"Hi, little baby," Sovanna cooed, picking Landon up. "You having fun?"

Leerah couldn't help but laugh when he nodded his head and smiled. Sovanna kissed his cheek and placed him down.

"Girl," Leerah said, huffing out a breath. "I am out of shape like shit."

Cackling, Sovanna said, "I see. You said not that many people RSVP'd. This looks like a lot of people to me."

She had to agree. The gift table was overflowing, and people were still trickling in. She glanced at the candy table and knew there wouldn't be enough bags for all the kids. The older ones would have to miss out. Leerah was beyond thankful for everyone showing up.

"I wasn't expecting this many people. Most of them are from his daddy's side."

Spotting Vee across the way, Leerah didn't plan on acknowledging her at all. She was still pissed about the conversation she sparked up at the daycare. When Vee waved and smiled, Leerah tossed her hand in the air, stiffly moving it from the right to the left, and that was it.

"I can't stand her. You remember she tried to play

me when I first found out I was pregnant?" Leerah asked.

Sovanna nodded. "Mhm. Terrance checked her so quick."

"Right. Talking about is he even his. Landon looks just like him."

Leerah heard her voice crack but tried to play it off. Sovanna caught on, though. She always did. Ready to pull her away from the crowd to get some time to herself, Sovanna looked her way.

"You okay?"

Clearing her throat, Leerah said, "Yeah. All of his siblings showed up. Well, most of them. A few are missing."

Terrance had a huge family, so she was happy to see most of them in attendance.

"How many does he have?" Sovanna asked.

Leerah laughed. "Too damn many. I think seven, or it might be eight. Their daddy was out here doing the most."

They laughed, and people watched for a few. When Sovanna spotted Terrance's first baby mama, Misha, she had to say something.

"I didn't know you invited Misha."

That would've never been in Leerah's plans had

she not matured since having Landon. Misha hadn't been one of her favorite people when she and Terrance first started dating. As the mother of his only and first daughter, she felt he should've tried to make it work with her. Misha fell back when he made it clear that they couldn't mess around anymore and meant it. She was shocked, to say the least, but eventually moved on and stopped starting arguments with Leerah.

"Yeah. She called herself reaching out to me after he passed and wanted to make amends… for the kids. No matter how I felt about Terrance, Landon deserves a relationship with his sister."

Sovanna nodded her head, loving how much Leerah had grown over the years. It was exhausting to see them almost come to blows and get into it every other week. Leerah decided that if Misha could be cordial for the sake of the children, so could she.

Sovanna nudged her shoulder. "Look at you growing up. I'm proud of you."

Leerah smirked. "Thank you, thank you. You know I've been trying to change my crazy ways."

Sovanna told her to keep it up and then cooed when she noticed Landon posing with Cree. Leerah had been staring at them before Sovanna acknowledged them. She'd been meaning to reach out and thank him for paying up daycare but it slipped her mind.

Leerah's eyes were already on them. She watched as they took a few more pictures, and she shook her head when he dug into his pocket, pulling out a hundred-dollar bill. Cree pointed to where they were standing, and Landon took off running, with him not too far behind. Before she could stop herself, Leerah let her intrusive thoughts spill from her mouth.

"Damn," she mumbled, taking in Cree's frame as he approached them.

She didn't mean to let the word slip but couldn't help herself. Cree's dark chocolate skin looked delectable and moisturized even from afar. His khaki shorts that extended past his knees offered her a view of his long legs. The left one was covered in ink and looked like a leg sleeve.

For as long as Leerah had known him, Cree had been on the thin side, but he was lean and muscular. His muscles were subtly defined rather than bulky, and she figured that was from his years of being a track and field athlete back in the day. She wondered what his workout routine was now because the way the black Prada t-shirt stretched across his torso should've been a sin. His trim waist complemented his six-foot-three stature, making Leerah's thoughts even more lewd.

She just knew he had...

Leerah fidgeted, shifting her stance as he approached. She'd never felt a way about Cree, even in college, but something in the air had her looking at him in a different light. His taper fade with a precise line-up looked so good paired with his goatee and close-cut beard. The hair was trimmed low enough for his chiseled jawline to become Leerah's primary focus.

When Cree flexed his jaw, Leerah's stomach tightened as if he had control of her insides, and he could've with the way she was unashamedly gawking at his handsomeness. The structure of his face was a work of art. It was a masterpiece, a one-of-one collector's edition with the dreamiest, dark brown eyes that made you feel at peace with one glance. His protruding Adam's apple made him even more attractive. Cree had earned tens across the board.

"What up. 'Preciate the invite," Cree said coolly, breaking Leerah's concentration.

He pulled her into a quick hug before giving Sovanna one as well. Leerah wanted to roll her eyes at his exclamation but knew it wouldn't matter. He was one of the first people on the list when she sent out invites. Whether he was first on it or last, Cree was still appreciative. He considered every moment in life a privilege because, to him, it was.

"Now, you know you didn't even need one," Leerah replied, grabbing the money from Landon's hand and placing it inside her back pocket.

The scowl on his face was the cutest as he looked up at Cree for some help.

"Nephew ain't feeling you pocketing his money."

Leerah shrugged. If she didn't pocket it, he'd lose it, and she'd hate to have to curse one of these folks out for stealing her baby's money. One of Landon's cousins ran over, and Leerah told him to go play. He had all day to be up under her and she wanted him to enjoy himself. She knew he'd be good and worn out by the time the party ended.

"Bro would've loved this. You hooked nephew up," Cree acknowledged.

Leerah swallowed the lump in her throat and nodded. "Yeah... thank you," she said.

For the sake of her emotional state, she was thankful that he didn't mention Terrance again. Instead, his gaze fell on the food table, contemplating what he'd fill his plate with. Cree licked his dark, soft lips and faced her.

"You ate?"

She shook her head. "I will in a little bit."

"A'ight. Make sure you do that," he said, nodding once.

Before she could check him for trying to regulate her eating habits, Cree walked off, leaving a trail of his woody-hedione scent behind. His smell almost awakened Leerah's inner hoe. She wanted to tell him to come back so she could just sniff him. Since she couldn't do that without looking and sounding crazy, she huffed a dramatic breath of relief. Sovanna could've snapped her neck the way she drew it back to look at her. The two of them had just carried on as if she wasn't standing there.

Sovanna leaned her way and whispered, "Um. Okay. It looks like you have some explaining to do because, ma'am... what the hell was that?"

Leerah had the same questions. "I honestly do not know."

Her answer was somewhat of a fib but more of the truth than anything. With them having been friends since senior year of college, Leerah shouldn't have been surprised by Cree's generosity. He was a giver—a provider. Not just monetary, either. Cree's the type of man you didn't have to ask to do something... he just did it. Naturally, he stepped up, and that wasn't going to change because they'd gotten older or because the one person who seemingly kept them linked was gone.

The type of time she thought he was on was a misjudgment from a place Leerah wasn't fond of. Her vulnerability had blurred the lines between them, and the temptation to cross it was heavier than ever. It'd only been four months since Terrance passed, and Leerah knew it had to be grief that caused her to be thinking this way. There was no other explanation. At least not one she could logically explain.

Leerah's eyes ventured toward the entrance. She or Sovanna couldn't believe people were still entering. When she saw the black AMG Benz remote-controlled SUV enter and Zahir, Terrance's brother, controlling it, Leerah laughed. Landon ran straight to it. Beside her, Sovanna was hyperventilating, not believing her eyes. Leerah was so engrossed with watching Landon trying to climb in the truck that she almost didn't hear Sovanna ask how Zahir knew them.

"Who?" Leerah questioned, snaking her neck in her direction.

"The...the man who's controlling the car."

Leerah waved her hand nonchalantly. "Oh.

That's one of Terrance's brothers on his daddy's side."

When Sovanna asked his name, Leerah began to think something was wrong. Her voice lowered a few octaves as if she didn't want to say the next words, and Leerah couldn't believe her. She knew for a fact she hadn't just said she had a one-night stand with Landon's uncle. By the look on her face, fluttering lashes as if blinking would make him disappear, Leerah knew she'd heard her correctly.

"Uh, hello!" Leerah trilled, snapping her fingers in her face.

Sovanna came back to reality. "Yeah, yeah. What's wrong?"

Leerah sucked her teeth. "You gon' sit here and act like I didn't hear what you just said? *He's* mystery dick?"

Sovanna's eyes widened as she shushed her. "Quiet down! Yes, that's him. Oh, my gosh. How fucking embarrassing."

Leerah thought the complete opposite. She didn't find this moment shameful but more so funny. It was just her best friend's luck to have given up the goodies to someone she knew and was very fond of. Knowing Sovanna, she was only embarrassed because she thought she'd never see him again.

Which made sense. However, Leerah wondered why she hadn't told her it was Zahir.

"Because I knew who he was," Sovanna replied smartly. "I never told you his name."

Humming, Leerah said, "True. But whatever. Let's go say hi. If you be nice, maybe he'll let you call him daddy again."

Laughing, she grabbed ahold of Sovanna's hand, leading her straight into the hands of a real man. Sovanna's ex wasn't worth a damn, and Leerah could say with the utmost confidence that Zahir would be just what Sovanna needed. From how he whispered in her ear and pulled her close, Leerah knew it'd be no time before Sovanna gave in.

While her uncles and cousins gathered everyone so they could sing happy birthday, Leerah and Terrance's mama, Andrea, made eye contact as she approached the table. She gave her a smile that, over the last few months, had been forced. Andrea was happy today, though. Her grandson was a daily reminder of her son in every way.

"Hey, honey. What do you need me to do?" Andrea asked, placing a hand on Leerah's back.

"Nothing as of right now, but probably pass out pieces of cake once it's cut."

"Okay. I can do that," she said as Landon reached for her.

On the days when he wasn't at daycare, Andrea had him by her side. It'd been like that before Terrance passed, but now she called Leerah almost every day to check on them and stop by the house. Landon grinned up at her while patting her cheeks with both hands.

"Hey, Nana's baby. I can't believe you're one," Andrea said.

"Dada, Dada," Landon cooed.

Hearing him say the word wasn't new, but it brought an onset of sorrow that Leerah had tried to contain all day. Her eyes pricked with unshed tears, and before she could muster up the strength to stop them from falling, they dripped down her face. Needing a second to herself, she rushed from behind the cake table and to the restroom.

Opting for the family bathroom for some privacy, she locked the door after entering. Leerah's chest heaved as she cried into the palms of her hands. Breaking down in front of everyone wasn't in her plans, but it was inevitable. Terrance's presence was terribly missed, and her baby knew it. Landon felt his absence just like she did.

Exhaling a deep breath, Leerah fanned her face. "Okay, okay. Get it together, girl. It's your baby's day."

Her tears didn't care about those mumbled words; they kept falling. Leerah didn't think it was possible to produce anymore. As days drifted by, turning into weeks that became months, she realized that there wasn't a cap to grief. Beyond Terrance being an amazing father, he was a friend of hers. A son, a brother, a cousin, an uncle, a good friend, and a man who didn't deserve to get his life taken by a reckless, drunk driver.

Entering the stall, she grabbed enough toilet paper to blow her nose and wipe her face. The woman staring back at her in the silver-trimmed mirror wasn't the one Leerah knew. Pieces of her had been buried with Terrance, and she wasn't sure whether that was a good thing or not. She became numb to many things, especially people. Her tolerance was at an all-time low, her attitude some days at an extreme high, and if she didn't have the support system she did, Leerah was sure she would've fallen into a state of depression.

Once she pulled herself together as best as she could, Leerah unlocked the door and pulled it open. The last person she expected to see waiting on her was Cree, yet there he was, posted up against the wall. Leerah cleared her throat, not knowing what to say.

"I just left everyone out there waiting." She chuckled nervously.

"And they gon' keep waiting until you're good."

She'd always loved the sound of his voice and how he never seemed to rush his words. It was warm and soothing, with a low, rumbled drawl and accent showcasing his Southern roots. Oklahoma, to be specific. He was an attentive listener more than anything, though, and Leerah didn't have to use any words for him to catch on.

She swallowed hard, eyes blinking quickly as she batted her damp lashes.

"We're on your time, so take as much as you need."

Her head tilted upwards, struggling to keep those stupid fucking tears at bay. If no one had checked on her, Leerah would've been fine. But, of course, he did. Cree always did, and it made Leerah lower her head to look at him. Sniffling, she waited for his expression to change from unbothered patience to annoyance. It never did. Instead, his eyes washed over her with concern. The type that angered Leerah because... why?

"You don't have to do the things you're doing,

Cree," she said with an unintentional bite in her tone that didn't move him.

She wasn't going to bring up him paying for daycare. He knew exactly what she was talking about.

"The man I am isn't letting you do this alone. You know me better than that."

Frustrated with her feelings, Leerah shook her head. "But I don't need you to."

"It doesn't matter what you think I need to do. I am. So, tell me how you would like me to show up for you since what I'm doing isn't to your satisfaction."

Leerah squeezed her eyes shut. *This man*, she thought and sighed from the depths of her soul. It was crying out for some clarity.

"What you're doing and have been doing is more than enough. It always has been. Thank you for real. I don't want you to think I'm being ungrateful."

"I'd never think that," Cree said smoothly.

"Good, because it's not that. I'm just... I'm not sure how to feel, especially today, so I'm all over the place."

Cree bobbed his head forward once. "Long as you feel something."

He didn't need her to explain herself. At least not

right now. That wasn't his intention when he stopped Sovanna from coming to check on her and came instead. Their close-knit friendship during the last year of college had shifted. It altered the second Cree brought Leerah around Terrance. That was almost four years ago, and they hadn't been the same since. It was shifting again, and so many factors played a role in why. Only Cree was clueless about them, while Leerah tried not to lay them out in his face.

"I'ma give you a pass, but I want an answer by next week," he said, smirking.

Leerah smiled. "I hear you."

"Good, 'cause I meant it when I said I got you. You and Landon. Know that," he said with earnest.

Leerah wanted to believe him, but her faith in anyone these days was scarce. So, she gave him a tight, forceful smile instead of responding. Stepping her way, Cree placed the sweetest kiss against her forehead. Leerah's heart fluttered before melting into a mess of what the hell. He'd always done that but hadn't since she and Terrance had gotten together. With him now gone, she wondered if their friendship would return to normal.

There's nothing normal about having a crush on

your deceased baby daddy's godbrother, she said to herself, leading them back to the gymnasium.

"LORD, WHEN IS IT MY TURN?"

THREE

After a long day of work, sitting in the car was so therapeutic. On days like today, Leerah needed it. She knew once they got out and went into the house, there'd be a million and one things to do, and Landon would be on ten. His last nap at daycare gave him more energy than ever. With him in the backseat chilling, waiting for them to get out, Leerah's eyes were glued to her phone.

Terrance's first baby mama, Misha, sent her a screenshot that made Leerah roll her eyes so hard they could've gotten stuck. Misha was cool, and they had a decent relationship, but Leerah wasn't buddy-buddy with her. The only people she liked to sit up and gossip with were Sovanna and Nae or her messy cousins, who stayed calling her with tea. She was surprised they hadn't sent her the screenshot first.

Today marked the fifth month since Terrance passed, and the woman he had in the car with him who survived couldn't help but express her feelings. Leerah knew all about Ashley but didn't care to keep up with her and never had. Misha, on the other hand, stayed on her page. Leerah was surprised she hadn't gotten blocked like she did. She hadn't done anything to the girl but exist and have a child with her quote-unquote man.

I never used to dread the 18th of every month, but I do now. It's been five months exactly since you left me, and I'm still so heartbroken, T. I miss you beyond words. If I could rewind the hands of time and change what happened that night, I would, but I can't & it hurts so bad. Some days I blame myself for even having us get out the house, but I know you wouldn't want that. I'ma try to only cry once today, but you know how I get when that liquor in my system lol. Love you forever, baby. Keep watching over me.

Reading the second to last sentence over, Leerah shook her head. Ashley loved a man who, days prior, had confessed his love to her. Terrance had been practically begging for his family back, yet was laid up with another woman forty-eight hours later. Men and their audacity. Leerah had only rolled her eyes so hard because she didn't know what Misha expected her response to be after seeing the status.

"The girl has a right to feel how she does," Leerah mumbled, locking her phone.

She didn't bother to respond. No response was one. For Misha to send her that today of all days was exactly why Leerah stayed to herself and cut people off. Instead of reaching out to see how she was doing, which she didn't expect, she came with the mess. Leerah didn't have time for that. It didn't make it any better that Ashley had attached multiple photos of her and Terrance. Pictures that told a story of two people who were obviously close. Had she not known about her, seeing that status would've had her sick to her stomach.

Instead, Leerah climbed out of the car, wondering what his last thoughts were before the crash. She read somewhere that some people knew when they were about to die, but she didn't know how accurate that was. She was just glad that Terrance didn't have to suffer for long. After getting Landon out of his car seat, the duo headed inside. As soon as they entered the house, Landon took off toward his room.

"He's about to pull all of them damn toys out," Leerah concluded, already knowing her baby.

She hadn't unboxed or put together nearly enough of his toys from the birthday party. The majority were stacked in his room, while the bigger ones, including his Benz, were at her mama's house. She'd tried to unbox one a day when they got home, but that task became a thing of the past.

After stripping out of her work clothes and into some cotton lounge shorts and a cami, Leerah cut Landon's TV on Ms. Rachel. Between her and Gracie's Corner, plus the learning toys and books he had, Landon was learning everything plus more for his age. Watching him play with the plastic balls from the playpen tent Sovanna bought him, Leerah smiled.

"You gon' let Mommy cook us dinner while you play?" she asked.

Landon shook his head no, making her laugh.

"Why not? I know you want to eat."

Since he started eating solid food, she mainly breastfed him at night before bed. Now that he was more active, he began to thin out and not keep much weight on him. He was still growing steadily, so

Leerah wasn't too concerned. Spotting his sippy cup nearby, Landon picked it up and held it out to her.

"Come on. Let's go get you some water."

He followed behind her into the kitchen and found pots to play with while she washed her hands before pouring him some ice-cold water. Leerah didn't know if it was because that's all she drank while pregnant, but her baby loved it.

"Ahh." The little noise he made, as if he'd just quenched his thirst, had Leerah cracking up.

"Oh my gosh." She giggled. "What you know about some ahh? I wish I could've recorded you."

Landon giggled with her before taking another sip. As she grabbed ingredients from the fridge, he found himself occupied with pulling bottles of water out of the plastic they came in. Leerah let him have at it. Once the water was boiled, she sprinkled in some salt and broke the noodles in half before dropping them in the pot. After spraying and rinsing off her bell peppers, she propped her phone against the flour canister and called Sovanna back on FaceTime. She had missed her call while driving.

"Hello. How can I help you today?" Sovanna answered.

"Girl, don't answer your phone like I'm bothering you." Leerah laughed, making Sovanna do the same.

"Maybe you are."

"That's too bad, hoe. What you doing?" Leerah asked.

"Nothing. At Zahir's, waiting for him to get home."

Leerah smirked. "That man really gave you the code to his home and his phone. I need to step my pussy up or something."

Sovanna cackled. "He iced my ears and wrists out, too."

She flashed her wrists in the camera before turning her head from left to right. Leerah placed the knife down and clapped, making Landon join her. Laughing, she picked him up so he could see her.

"Tell your g-mommy we're proud of her."

Landon smiled wide, making Sovanna poke her bottom lip out. "Hey, Stink. Look at all those teeth. And you were worried about them not coming in."

"I sure was. They popped up out of nowhere a few days after his birthday."

"Like they were supposed to. What y'all eating for dinner?"

Leerah put Landon down and continued chopping the peppers. "Spaghetti and garlic bread. Something quick and easy."

"Ooh," Sovanna cooed. "That sounds good. It'd be even better with some fish."

"Yeah, you're right, but I didn't feel like thawing any out and frying it. Maybe tomorrow. You know the spaghetti be hitting way more the second day."

Nodding, Sovanna chuckled. "Hell yeah. Save me a bowl. I'll come by to get it and to chill tomorrow."

Leerah told her okay and then got quiet for a few seconds. "I can't believe it's been five months."

Sovanna's stomach bubbled with discomfort at her words. She was waiting for Leerah to bring up today's date like she had every month since he passed.

"How you feeling?" she asked softly, letting her know she didn't have to divulge if she didn't want to.

It was a best-friend thing—the tone, the question. Some days, she was good and didn't have to ask because Leerah would straight up tell her. On other days, Leerah appreciated the questions because not talking about him hurt, too.

"I couldn't really sleep last night and my chest was hurting earlier. Saw some shit that I probably wouldn't have had Misha not sent it to me."

Sovanna sucked her teeth. "What did she send you?"

"The girl's status he was with that night. She misses him just like everybody else."

Leerah rolled her eyes. She had nothing against the girl but now hated that she saw Terrance in a negative light. Had he not been moving the way he had with her nights before, Leerah knew she wouldn't have had any physical reaction. Mentally, she couldn't wrap her mind around him blowing smoke up her ass about getting his shit together. And the fact that he was no longer here made it worse because she had plans to give him another chance once Monday morning came.

"That's... a crazy position to be in. Why did Misha even send you that?" Sovanna asked.

"Your guess is as good as mine. I'm not about to sit up and discuss the next bitch, especially with someone who is cool with a lady who doesn't like me."

Leerah would never. She couldn't see Misha running her business down to Vee, but then again, she wouldn't put it past her.

"Yeah, that's crazy. If she's willing to run her mouth about that girl with you, you already know she gon' do it about you."

Leerah dropped the peppers into the hot, oiled

pan. "Exactly. Aht! Put that down," she scolded, making Landon flinch and drop the vase in his hand.

Thankfully, it was a heavy-duty one she picked up from HomeGoods, so it didn't break.

"What he got?" Sovanna asked.

"Girl, the vase I showed you yesterday. He's too strong picking this up. Let me see your muscles."

He laughed as she helped him flex his arm and squeezed his non-existent muscle.

"Oooh. You so strong." Sovanna grinned.

"Go get one of your toys. Don't play with this, okay?"

Landon moseyed out of the kitchen, stopping to pick up a toy truck. He listened when he wanted to.

"You really had a baby," Sovanna said, still in disbelief.

Leerah chuckled. "I say that every day. Be looking back at pictures from when I was pregnant, like damn. I really got caught slipping."

Laughing, they both shook their heads.

"No, seriously. I feel like had I not been in Houston, that wouldn't have happened." Sovanna squinted her eyes, waiting for her to decline her remark.

"Yeah, okay." Leerah laughed. "It was bound to

happen. You know fucking raw and everything. I'm sure you know all about that, Ms. Cream Pie."

Sovanna cackled. "You're never going to let me live that down, are you?"

"Nope. But I love that for you, with your freaky ass. Zahir introduced you to some grown man dick, huh?"

"Sure did. Making me want to spend the rest of my life with him." Sovanna giggled, meaning every word.

"Whew. Lord, when is it my turn?"

Sovanna cocked her head to the side. "It could be your turn any moment. I know the perfect person, too."

"Girl, who?" Leerah asked incredulously, snaking her neck. "I know you ain't been holding up the prayer line asking God to send me one of those lames niggas who been in my inbox lately."

"What have they been saying?" Sovanna laughed.

"Nothing worth responding to. All they have to offer is sympathy dick that probably ain't even big or good enough to cry over or on. Please." Leerah huffed, using her meat masher to cook the ground turkey.

Landon clung to her side, whining to be picked up. After so long, he wanted some attention.

"Well, you'll never know unless you take that risk. Buuut," Sovanna dragged. "I wasn't talking about them. I was talking about Cree. Don't think I forgot."

"E," Landon said excitedly. His eyes lit up hearing his name.

"See. Even he knows what's up."

Leerah picked him up and loved on him with hugs and kisses before placing him in his highchair. Grabbing a bowl of cut-up fruit from the fridge, she put some on his tray.

"Ain't nothing up. I don't know why you insist on making us something it can never be."

"What'd you tell me I was being that day? Too chicken to face Zahir like a woman? That's exactly how you're acting."

Leerah wasn't trying to hear any of that. "Call it what you want. Just because he paid Landon's daycare for three months and—"

"Wait. When did he do that?" Sovanna questioned. This was news to her.

"I forgot to tell you. It was like last month. I didn't even know until Vee mentioned it and tried questioning me why he did it. Like I'm supposed to know."

Sovanna went silent. She had a few ideas why.

"What?" Leerah huffed. "Not you thinking the same thing as that wobble-wig head lady."

Snorting, Sovanna laughed. "Wobble-wig is fucking hilarious. Leave that woman alone."

"Nope. Tell her to mind her business, and I will. Now, what? He can't pay for daycare out of the kindness of his heart as my friend?"

"I mean, yes. Cree has always been a giver, but do you think he's trying to replace Terrance?"

Sovanna spoke lowly, almost as if she didn't want to ask the question, but she had to know. She had to keep it all the way real with Leerah because she'd do the same. Truthfully, Leerah had been thinking the same thing.

"Replace him in what capacity because Terrance was a damn good daddy."

Nodding, Sovanna said, "He definitely was. I'll give him that. So, that only leaves one other space to fill. Well, two." She smirked.

Leerah twisted the top off the jar of sauce and shook her head. "Nope. Those spaces are closed and never reopening."

"Well, that sucks. I know you need some dick."

Leerah flipped her off. She was right, though. It had been way too long since she'd gotten some, but that wasn't a conversation she was ready to have.

"Shoutout to Cree, though. Free daycare for three months is a blessing," Sovanna said.

"Tell me about it. If I had me a little boo and he came through like that, I would've shown him how appreciative I was with my throat."

The truth was that Leerah wanted to express her deepest throat gratitude to Cree. It was one of the reasons she had to keep looking away from him that day in the hallway outside of the bathroom. Had she not, she would've sucked him off until snot was running from her nose and her eyes were leaking happy tears.

"Okay, I heard that." Sovanna laughed.

Just as Leerah began mixing the sauce and meat, a hard knock came from the front door. Her eyes darted to the time on the stove, and her face screwed up. She wasn't expecting anyone but knew that Andrea and her mama liked to pop up on her.

"Watch him right quick so I can see who this is," she said, placing the spoon down.

Happily, Sovanna talked to Landon while Leerah headed to the front door. *Maybe it's UPS or Amazon,* she thought. Leerah wasn't aware of the many stages of grief, but she called this one big spender. Every time a wave of sadness hit her, she was online shopping for her and Landon. The heaviness in her chest eased away with each purchase and shipping notification.

Peeking out of the peephole, Leerah's eyes bulged before whispering in a hiss, "Oh my gosh. We don' spoke this man up."

Cree stood on the other side of her door looking fine as ever, and he hadn't come empty-handed. Twisting the locks, Leerah pulled it open. Wonderment crossed her face as she eyed the gift and grocery bags from Target in his hand. Noticing her hesitance, Cree smiled, and Leerah wanted to fall out.

"What's up? Can I come in?"

FOUR

Cree entered her home and moved around like he lived there. Stunned, Leerah slowly closed the door and locked it. She took in how comfortable he seemed as he began removing things from the bags and placing them on her dining table. *What the hell is going on right now?*

"Um, hello," Leerah said curiously, crossing her arms over her breasts.

Cree faced her. "Why you greet me like that?"

"I'm just a lil' confused by your presence. What're you doing here?"

"You made a tweet about needing help putting Landon's toys together, so I came to help you out."

Leerah wasn't prepared for his answer. She blinked slowly, thinking back to Sovanna's question about him trying to fill a space that wasn't meant to be filled.

"Where he at?" Cree questioned.

His question snapped her out of her daze, and her feet started moving. "In the kitchen."

Before returning to the kitchen, she snagged a shirt from the basket of clean clothes by the couch and slid it over her head. Cree held back from asking how her day was. She looked good and comfortable in the booty shorts and Nirvana graphic tee. His eyes darted to her thighs but quickly left them. Temptation was a motherfucker, but Cree had admirable restraint.

There was no way he couldn't help but steal a peek at her smooth, brown thighs. They were thick and juicy, just as Cree loved them on a woman. Instead, he focused on the back of her head, where an amass of curls were secured in a slick ponytail—one of her favorite, quick go-to styles.

"Lando," Cree said, entering the kitchen. "She got you locked down, my boy. What you in here eating on?"

His eyes lit up as he extended his hand covered in mashed strawberries and grapes.

"You better take it, too." Leerah chuckled.

"Nah. Hand me this one," Cree instructed,

pointing to a diced strawberry he hoped hadn't been slobbered on.

Landon picked it up with the same messy hand and handed it to him. Happily, Cree popped it into his mouth.

"Mmm. That was good, man. Thank you."

Landon just smiled, and Leerah had to stop herself from screaming when Sovanna made her presence known.

"Heeey, Cree!" she spoke louder than she should have on purpose.

His head swiveled before he chucked his chin up. "What up, Vanna."

"Nothing much. I guess I'm the only one who didn't get an invite to dinner, huh?"

Cree glanced at Leerah and shrugged. "I guess so. We'll save you a plate."

"Oh. How nice of you to think of me." Sarcasm dripped from her words, making Leerah playfully roll her eyes.

"Girl, don't even start. You laid up in that man's crib and probably already have dinner waiting for him," Leerah said, opening the box of garlic bread.

"Yep, I sure do. It's been marinating all day, actually."

Knowing she wasn't talking about any type of food, Leerah laughed.

"I can't stand you! Bye. We'll call you tomorrow."

Sovanna cracked up. "Talk to y'all later."

"Why didn't you invite her over for dinner with us?" Cree asked.

"Us?" She laughed. "You popped up, which by the way, is some shit you don't do with me. But you know that, right?"

A hint of a smirk teased his lips. "Sure."

"Sure, my ass. Where are you coming from anyway?"

"Work and the store. You need some help?"

She turned away from the stove after sliding the pan inside the oven. "Help cooking? No, I got it. The only thing left to prepare is the salad."

"A'ight. I'ma get him cleaned up and start putting his toys together. You wanna come let me know which ones you want to unbox?"

Leerah leaned against the counter and stared him down. There needed to be a study held for why Black men looked so damn good in the simplest of clothing. His black basketball shorts, a fresh, white Stafford shirt out the pack, and crisp white Forces made Leerah want him to stay in her face.

"Some of them need batteries," she said.

"I know. I bought some when I stopped at Target."

She smirked. "You just came all prepared, huh?"

"I tried to. Y'all needed something else?"

Leerah wanted to tell him that he should've brought some ice cream but she didn't. She was down to the last corner of her banana pudding flavor from Trader Joe's and was sad about it.

"No. And I can clean him up. You don't—"

"Lando, tell your mama I got this. She not running anything, is she?" Cree asked as he grabbed some paper towels.

He wiped the remaining fruit from the tray, tossing it in the trash. Running more paper towels under the faucet, he used a bit of Dawn soap before wringing it out and wiping Landon's hands and face. Leerah stood back, watching. Her gut twisted with guilt, but her heart felt less heavy.

Her poor heart. She didn't know if Cree was trying to mend it or steal it. Either one would've been fine, but neither option was safe. Cree swooped Landon out of his seat, running a hand over his curly hair.

"You ever think about loc'n him up when he gets older?" Cree asked.

Leerah shook her head. "No. So everyone can *really* tell me how much he doesn't look like me?"

He cracked a grin. "You right. Come on, Lando. Show me your room."

Landon looked at Leerah, and she nodded her head. "You can show him, baby. I'm right behind y'all."

He took off to his room, and Cree grabbed the bag off the table. It was Leerah's turn to admire him from the back, and she was glad they had to venture down a hallway so he couldn't see her slightly panicking. *This is too much,* she thought as they entered Landon's Sesame Street-themed room. She pointed out and grabbed which toys of his she wanted to be put together, and Cree got to work.

"You got a screwdriver?" Cree asked.

Leerah chuckled. "Um, probably around here somewhere. I have no idea where it'd be."

"I figured that. Grab that gift bag in there and come back in here."

Her brows dipped, but she did what he said. She made a pit stop in the kitchen first to stir the spaghetti and check on the bread that wasn't ready. Turning the stovetop on low, she went to grab the gift bag and frowned by its weight.

"What the hell does he have in here," Leerah grumbled, peeking inside.

All she saw was something pink and she smirked. Taking it to the bedroom, she set it beside Cree, who had his legs stretched wide with a toy in between them, while Landon destroyed her hard work of cleaning up from the night before.

"Open it," Cree instructed.

She untied the bow and pulled out a pink toolbox. Leerah couldn't hide her smile.

"This is too cute," she gushed. "You just knew I needed one of these, huh?"

"I wasn't wrong. Can you hand me the screwdriver, please?"

Opening the box, she located the correct tool with the pink and black handle and handed it to him. The set came equipped with screws, a measuring tape, a hammer, a lever, a box cutter, scissors, and many other tools Leerah knew would come in handy one day.

"Thank you," she said, fighting the urge to tell him that he didn't have to get her anything.

Cree knew it, too. He glanced at her and smirked. "You're welcome," he said just as a toy dinosaur, one of Landon's cousins got him, came to life.

When his eyes widened just as big as his smile,

Leerah knew it'd be his newest obsession. She watched him play for a few seconds before leaving out. The bread was done when she made it to the kitchen this time. Quickly, she grabbed the premade salad mix and dumped it into a bowl. Leerah didn't even know she was crying until her vision blurred, and she couldn't see the lettuce.

This time, they were tears of happiness. No matter how much of a fuss she made about Cree popping up, she was more than happy he did. Not wanting the bread to get cold, she went to get them so they could eat. Landon put up a fight, not wanting to leave his room and new toys.

"Nah, none of that. We gon' come back in here when you finish eating. You don't want to eat what your mama cooked?" Cree asked.

Landon shook his head, and Cree laughed.

"Well, I do. So, come on, lil' dude." He picked him up and carried him to the kitchen. "Where do y'all normally eat at?"

Leerah turned away from the plate she was fixing. "Him in his highchair so I can help him while I lean against the counter."

It wasn't that way every time they ate, but it was most of the time. If Landon were asleep or playing in his room, she'd be right in front of the TV in the living room.

"Finish fixing your plate and sit at the table. I got him."

Leerah sighed. "Cree."

"You got it smelling real good in here. Gon' head. I know what I'm doing."

But what are you really doing? Leerah wanted to scream. She was so used to doing and running things on her own that taking orders from him tested all her patience. When she didn't say anything, Cree walked over to her. Grabbing the paper plate off the counter, he piled two spoonfuls of spaghetti onto it.

"You want some more?" he asked.

Leerah shook her head, so he moved on to grab a piece of garlic bread and fix her a bowl of salad. Seeing that he wasn't letting her do a thing, Leerah decided to put herself to use and grab the ranch from the fridge. She sat at the dining table with Landon right by her side. She picked him up just as Cree placed her plate and bowl down.

"Let your mama eat in peace, lil' dude," he jested, removing Landon from her lap. "You need anything else?"

Leerah shook her head. "No. Thank you for fixing my food."

"You're welcome. I'ma grab ours right quick."

Cree fixed him a plate full of spaghetti that filled the entire thing, two pieces of garlic bread, and a bowl of salad. Grabbing one of Landon's bowls from the dishrack, he put some spaghetti inside it, breaking the noodles into smaller pieces. He grabbed them forks, a small blue plastic one for Landon, and sat at the table. He sat Landon on his left leg and made sure his bowl was out of reach for the moment.

"A'ight, put your hands together," Cree said, grabbing his tiny wrists and pressing his hands together.

Thinking they were about to start clapping, Landon patted his hands together.

"Yay," Leerah cheered, clapping with him. "You're going to say grace?"

Cree nodded. "Yeah. That coo' with you?"

She mumbled, "Mhm," and bowed her head, and he did the same.

"Lord, thank you for today and this food we are about to receive. Thank you for Leerah, as well. She must've known I was hungry. Continue to keep your hands around her and Landon. May her days get easier and her nights restful. She deserves that, and I know you can make it happen. Let this food be nourishing to our bodies in Jesus' name. Amen."

Clearing her throat full of unwanted emotions, Leerah said, "Amen."

Saying grace was one thing.

Having a man speak to God about you on his behalf was a different type of love that made Leerah want to cry. Cree did it so naturally that she wondered if it had been the first time. She watched them as Landon ditched his fork and ate with his hands. Cree wasted no time digging into his food, eyes focused like he'd missed something. He caught her gaze right before biting into his garlic bread.

"It's hitting if that's what you're wondering," Cree said, complimenting her cooking.

Leerah swallowed hard. "That's... that's not it."

"What's the matter?"

"Is that your first time praying for me?"

Cree shook his head. "No."

His answer was swift, leaving no room for Leerah to think otherwise. But then he added more words, lying to rest whatever wild thoughts were running through her mind, replacing them with what-ifs.

"I've prayed for you since the day I met you."

Cree's words would've knocked the wind out of

her had she been standing because Leerah felt weak. Vulnerable. His words were spoken with the utmost confidence as if he knew that years from when they'd met, she'd need those prayers. It spoke volumes about the type of man Cree was and spoke even louder about his heart. It was pure and golden.

When they finished eating, Cree put the rest of Landon's toys together while Leerah straightened up the kitchen. Before putting the spaghetti in a container, she placed some aside for Cree in a Tupperware container. The last piece of garlic bread was slid into a zip-lock bag. He hadn't asked for a to-go meal, but she knew he'd want some with the way he cleaned his plate.

Not wanting to intrude but needing to change Landon's diaper, she went to the room after cleaning up and watching TV for a little bit. Seeing how late it was getting, she needed to get ready to call it a night. Seeing Cree sitting in the rocking chair with Landon knocked out in his lap was the cutest sight ever. She knew there was a reason it had gotten so quiet.

Returning to the living room, Leerah grabbed her phone from the couch and crept back into the bedroom. Cree's head was leaned back with his eyes closed, and she had to snap a few pictures. When she got the ones she wanted, Leerah tapped his leg.

Protectively, his hand cradled Landon, and he peeled those dreamy eyes open.

"Someone's tired," Leerah said.

"Yeah. He must've had a long day."

She chuckled. "I'm talking about you. Here, let me get him changed and in bed."

Picking him up, Leerah rubbed his back as he started to whine and headed to her room. Since she couldn't bathe him tonight, she planned to put him in the shower with her in the morning. He loved the shower more than baths now, and that was just fine with her when they were pressed for time. After changing his diaper and turning rain sounds on through the Calm app on her phone, Leerah left, leaving the door cracked.

Cree gathered his belongings and placed the unused batteries in the kitchen's junk drawer. Spotting the to-go container, he looked her way.

"This for me?"

"Yes. You ate that plate like no one ever feeds you."

Smirking, he licked his lips. "No one has fed me that good in a while."

Leerah rubbed her neck and broke their eye contact. Downright filthy thoughts flooded her brain, and she needed to get him up out of her house before she fed him something he'd surely get addicted to.

"Thanks," she mumbled.

He grabbed his food, and they walked to the door.

"'Preciate you for allowing me in your presence today, Princess."

Leerah gasped, tossing a hand over her face as she giggled. "Oh my gosh. You haven't called me that in so long."

"Yeah... I know. It kinda slipped, but my bad."

He withdrew, remembering why he'd stopped calling her that in the first place. Terrance. When he realized that things were serious between them, when Leerah popped up pregnant, Cree cut all nicknames, friendly hugs, texts, phone calls, and visits out. Not completely, but enough to respect the boundaries he could no longer cross. Now... he felt like it was okay to place a foot over the line if she wanted him to.

"No, no. You're fine. I miss being called Princess Leerah. It has a nice ring to it," she said, grinning.

Hearing the nickname he'd given her in college fall from his lips felt like a thread of their shared past had reconnected, re-establishing a sense of normalcy between them.

"I bet. Look at you being all nice," he said.

Her stance shifted, poking her hip out, but Cree kept his eyes leveled. "I can be nice sometimes."

"I know that. I can be nice, too, if you let me without being combative."

Leerah huffed, feeling herself get emotional, and Cree stopped her from asking the question he knew was coming.

"Don't ask me why again after today. You deserve everything good in this world, and if that's me, let me be that for now."

"What about later? I don't deserve good shit later on in life?" she asked with a hint of humor in her voice.

Cree smirked, and she shoved his chest. His hand clasped around her wrist before she could lower it. Smile gone, Cree's eyes locked onto her with a suffocating intensity that made Leerah shiver internally.

"You do. And if that's what you want, you'll get it."

She wanted many things, specifically for Cree to stop touching her. Of course, he wasn't a mind reader; if he was, he ignored her thoughts. The kiss he placed on her forehead stole all her brain cells. That was the only logical explanation for what

Leerah did next. Tilting her head, she kissed Cree's soft lips. She would've kept them there, but Cree pulled away.

If he was stunned, he didn't show it. But he felt it, and so did his dick.

"Leerah," he said calmly, and she shook her head.

"I know. I'm sorry. I shouldn't have done that."

He exhaled sharply. "Yeah... I don't know. Don't trip. It's all good. I'ma head out. Thank you for dinner. I appreciate you."

Cree was talking faster than she'd ever heard him, and she wanted to laugh but held it in. He unlocked the door, stepped out, and told her to have a good night. Leerah told him to do the same and closed the door. She pressed a hand to her chest as her mouth dropped.

"Bitch. What did you just do?" she whispered and then squealed, "Oh my gosh. That nigga's lips are so damn soft."

Knock! Knock! Knock!

The knocks weren't loud but since she was right by the door still, Leerah jumped out of her body. With her heart racing, she swung the door open without checking to see who it was. Thankfully, it was Cree and not someone trying to bring her harm.

"Don't do that again," he chastised. "I could've been anybody."

Leerah gulped and mumbled, "You're right. I wasn't thinking."

I had your soft ass lips on my brain, boy. Duh! she thought, trying not to grin.

Cree dug in his pocket, retrieving five one-hundred-dollar bills and a fifty. "I forgot to lace Lando's pockets. That fifty is his; the rest is yours."

"Thank you, Cree. Let me know when you make it home."

He finally gave her body a full once-over, loving the glow of her warm brown complexion, curious brown eyes with a dark ring around the iris, a small nose with tiny nostrils, and those lips. They were luscious and had a curve that made it difficult for Cree to keep his lips to himself this time, but he did. He wanted to tug the bottom lip into his mouth and suck on it until she moaned his name.

What Leerah had just pulled erased the line drawn between them. She was a mystery to Cree now more than before. No longer was she an open book that he could delicately flip the pages of and get lost in—not yet, at least. She was similar to the hardback copy of Hassan by Nina on one of her bookshelves. Leerah was an exclusive edition you only got to experience if luck was on your side.

Cree didn't know this newly developed Leerah, but he wanted to. Seeing her as a mother shined a brighter, newer light on whom he had already grown to love as a friend.

"I will. Lock up," he said, leaving out again.

This time, Leerah locked the door and walked away but looked back as if she knew Cree had done the same thing. Having him fill one of those spaces Sovanna mentioned no longer sounded like the worst thing to do. If Leerah was being honest, it never had.

"YOUR FEELINGS ARE MORE INVOLVED
THAN BEFORE."

FIVE

Running a few games on the court always reminded Cree of how up in age he was getting. He didn't consider thirty-three old by far, but compared to a few youngsters in their mid-twenties, they'd given him a run for his money. Regulating his breaths, he wiped the sweat from his forehead with a towel and sat on the bench.

"Can't hang with them young niggas, huh?" Bostyn, a good friend and business partner of his, joked.

"Caught me on an off day," Cree countered before guzzling some water.

It'd been an off week, but he wasn't divulging that.

"That's gon' be your excuse next time?" Mario, one of his opponents, asked.

Cree shook his head. Mario barely put any points on the board, so he should've been the last one talking shit.

"You ain't got room to speak, cuz," Saleem asserted. "What you drop, five?"

"Nah, 'bout six."

The men cracked up.

"Clown," Synovi, one of the youngsters who'd given Cree a run for his money, said.

"Aye. Just 'cause you were out there hooping like your life was on the line, don't mean I had to," Mario said.

Synovi waved him off. "That's exactly why you ain't on my team next time."

"Aahh. This sore loser," Bostyn cracked. "It's all good, bro. Lunch on me. What y'all about to get into after this?"

The men had been meeting at the gym for the last year and a half. Some days, it was to work out, while other days, they ran the court. Cree's attendance had fallen off for over a month after Terrance passed, but he was getting back into the swing of things. Had he been here, Mario more than likely wouldn't have dropped any points.

"Head to the shopping center. Check on a few things," Cree answered.

Saleem nodded. "I meant to get with you about some ideas I had."

"You looking to expand?" Bostyn asked.

"Yeah. You got some properties?" Saleem asked.

Bostyn nodded. "I got a few in mind."

Cree owned a shopping center and was always open to hearing new ideas from his people. Bostyn was heavily involved in the real estate game, while Saleem had just opened his first juice bar inside the shopping center a few months ago. Cree knew Synovi through his cleaning business, whom he hired to clean the mall, and he knew Mario through Terrance. The time, effort, money, and dedication it took to operate a business on such a large scale didn't come easy.

At twenty-five, Cree invested in a struggling strip mall that, according to his grandfather, would be a significant investment in some years. He wasn't wrong. That was eight years ago, and his investment tripled. With a good amount of funds saved, a few loans, and eager business owners ready to expand, Cree had a lucrative shopping center in what was now considered the heart of the city. The location was a high-traffic area and would only continue to grow.

"A'ight. I'll hit you up in a few days," Saleem said as a woman entered the gym.

Her hunter-green two-piece set displayed her slim but thick dark brown skin, and Cree barely acknowledged her. He did notice the slight limp in her walk and the scars on her legs. She was here to see one person, and he hoped she didn't try to hold a conversation with him. He had nothing to say.

"Hey, y'all," Ashley spoke, waving.

"What up."

"What's good."

Saleem and Bostyn were the only two to speak, while Cree and Synovi gave subtle head nods.

"Good looking out, sis," Mario said as she handed him a set of keys. "Where you coming from?"

She broke the stare she was giving Cree. "The house. Stop leaving your shit over there. Thank you."

Mario waved her off. "Whatever. You going to Mama's later?"

"Mhm," she answered. "Bye."

Cree's attention was on his phone, responding to

a text message when Ashley stood in front of him. He flexed his jaw as he glanced up.

"How have you been?" she asked.

"Why?"

Her mouth opened and closed. "I...I was just wondering, is all. You have this secret animosity toward me like I did something."

"That's a trait of a woman. If you feel that way, I don't know what to tell you." Cree shrugged.

"He was single, you know. What happened was very unfortunate for both of us."

Cree's pensive stare made Ashley wish she would've kept walking.

"Yeah, it was, and so is it for his kids," Cree said.

In his eyes, had Ashley never called Terrance to come and get her that night, he would've still been alive. He wasn't blaming her for his demise, but Cree couldn't help but wonder what if. There was no secret animosity or hatred for Ashley on his end because he didn't know her, nor did he care about her and Terrance's relationship. It no longer existed.

Ashley blinked back tears and swallowed the boulder in her throat. "Yeah, I know," she acknowledged, touching her stomach.

Before Cree could react, she exited the gym. All the men had been conversing, but Cree knew they were ear-hustling, especially Mario because he was the first to say something.

"What's up with you and my sister?"

Cree slowly turned his head. "Nothing. I don't know her."

"Sounded like she had a problem with you."

"That's a her problem. If she did have one with me, you gon' handle it? Don't be trying to press me about no woman that ain't mine," Cree said calmly and stood up.

Mario hiked his shorts up. "What you standing up for?"

"Nigga, so I can leave and not beat your ass for talking to me like you missing some brain cells. Hiking your shorts up like you about to do something." He scoffed, slapping hands with Bostyn, Synovi, and Saleem. He scowled at Mario, wanting him to say something else slick, but he didn't. "I'm out."

Tossing the strap of his gym bag over his shoulder, Cree exited the gym. He was no longer in the mood to be around people but work still had to be done. Climbing in his truck, his mind ventured to Ashley and the hand she placed on her stomach. He wasn't lying when he said he didn't know her, so he had no clue what she was insinuating by doing that.

"She can't be pregnant," Cree said aloud, pulling out of the parking lot.

It'd been months, and her stomach would've been showing by now if she were. Cree minded the businesses that paid him, so he stayed out of other people's. As a man and Leerah's friend, seeing Terrance mess around on her with other women had always gotten under his skin. Watching her go from a goofy dean-list college girl who liked to enjoy life and pour it into others to an aggressive, quick-tempered, callous woman Cree didn't recognize was crazy.

Being in a relationship with Terrance had more downs than ups. At some point, Cree tuned Terrance out whenever he would bring Leerah's name up. Leerah hardly mentioned him, feeling that sharing their business with his godbrother was inappropriate, but Cree knew everything wasn't kosher. Terrance had dimmed her light when Cree knew she was meant to only ever shine bright around this motherfucker; no matter who didn't like it.

It was a sticky situation, and Cree was uncomfortable most days. Somehow, they'd place him in the middle of some of their arguments. Right was right, and wrong was wrong in his eyes. He didn't base decisions on scattered emotions, but on his heart and gut, so he always gave it to them straight. He wondered if the same should apply to Leerah after seeing Ashley. Keeping that from her would heavily weigh on him, but he also didn't want to stir the pot if she was fronting about being pregnant or having been.

Either way, Cree now had that situation and Leerah on his mind. *Still.* She hadn't left it since that night at her place. He meant every word he told her and always had. He couldn't brush off her kissing him like he'd done other things, but he needed to. He had to. It was disrespecting his boy on all levels, and that wasn't who Cree was trying to be.

But Leerah... with her vulnerable, needy eyes and alluring personality, was making it difficult for him to stay on the straight and narrow. She was trying, though. His texts had been ignored for five days straight, and Cree was ready to pull up on her. He told her everything was good, and he thought she agreed, but clearly, she hadn't.

When he reached the shopping center, Cree pulled up their text thread and began typing a message but then deleted it. Instead, he sent her a voice note so she could understand how he was really feeling. While Leerah appreciated his presence that day, he was grateful for her allowing him in their space. Mentally, he knew it could be a lot.

"What's up, Princess? How your day going? I see you still ignoring me like I did something wrong. That's coo'. I'ma let you get over whatever embarrassment you might be feeling but ain't no need for any. You did what was on your heart, and you always should. You wanna know what's on my heart right now? How many minutes it'd take me to get to your job. That's crazy talk, huh? Something you probably not used to hearing from me but... shit. I guess a few things have changed. I know you gon' listen to this and not respond, but as long as you hear me I'm good with that. Tell Lando I said what's up and enjoy the rest of your day."

He tapped the red square to end the recording before tapping the blue arrow to send it. Slightly smirking, he hopped out of the truck. Leerah was going to hear him one way or another. She could only ignore him for so long until her resolve crumbled. With one task accomplished, Cree headed inside the shopping center to finish some work. He had a new tenant moving in next week and wanted to ensure everything went smoothly.

His grandparents' house was Cree's second home. He stopped by on days like today when he just wanted to watch TV and catch up with the man who raised him. They talked every other day, but Cree made it his duty to lay eyes on him at least three times a week.

"You got a lot on your mind," Gramps said.

Cree glanced away from the true crime documentary that was admittedly watching him. "You're asking me?"

"You know I ain't asking."

Cree chuckled. Nothing could get past Cole Landry, affectionately known as Gramps. He sensed his grandson's off-putting energy the second he entered the home. Now, he needed to know what had him so bothered and out of his element.

"Nothing for you to be worried about," Cree assured.

Gramps waved him off and took a swig of his ice-cold beer from the can. "Probably not, but humor your old man. Everything good with the shopping center?"

Cree nodded. "Yes, sir. You were right all those years ago."

Gramp's smirk wasn't one of cockiness. He was proud of Cree for taking the leap of faith and putting his money into a business that would continue to flourish. His contribution played a role in obtaining the property as well, but Gramps gave him all the credit.

"I've never steered you wrong. Now, talk," Gramps demanded sternly.

Cree scratched his head before stroking his waves. "You ever did the right thing, but it was still wrong?"

"Yep. Plenty of times in my life. Right in my eyes, but perceived as wrong by others."

"That's where I'm at with a situation," Cree divulged.

"I didn't raise you to care what folks think."

"And I don't, but I'm thinking of the overall consequences of my actions. There are a lot of people involved that could be hurt in the process. I just want to make my intentions clear."

Gramps nodded, fully understanding, but he wanted Cree to understand something as well.

"This about Leerah and her boy, huh?"

Cree chuckled. "You don't miss a thing, do you?"

"You don't miss much when you've lived this long."

"True. Would I be wrong for stepping up?"

"Are you a man?"

Cree answered without hesitance. "Yes, sir."

"Well, then. There's your answer. Grown men take care of what they love. They take care of the home even if it wasn't theirs to begin with but made it theirs. If you're in it for the wrong reasons, I think I'd raised a fool."

Cree cracked a smile. "You didn't. You and Granny did a stellar job if you ask me."

The mention of his late wife put a smile on Gramps' face. Minnie Landry was the sweetest woman ever. She was a beacon of love and care, devoted to her husband, and a grandmother who didn't play when it came to Cree. Though she was no longer here, having passed away when Cree was twenty-eight, her warmth was still evident in and out of the home.

When Cree's mother, Veronica, prioritized her modeling career over being a mother, Gramps and Minnie didn't hesitate to step up to the plate and raise him. Cree's father had been in and out of his life like a picture that faded over time. He was exposed for his lack of fatherly duties, handling the opportunities he was given to be a father without care, which resulted in forfeiting all possibilities of restoring their relationship.

Cree was grateful he didn't make an effort to be in his life. Forcing someone to do something they didn't want to do would always end in turmoil. He held no resentment for his mother, either. Not as an adult, anyway. She chose her career over her child, and there wasn't anything Cree could do about it. He loved her no less but knew how much to give her.

His grandparents created a legacy of love that resonated through him, though it'd skipped their daughter. Being nurtured with love created an environment for Cree to become the man he was today. There was never a moment where he didn't feel as if he couldn't express himself, cope with adversities thrown his way, take on new challenges, and grow overall as a man. So, this new venture with Leerah had him questioning everything he was.

"We did our best," Gramps said. "So, what's the game plan?"

"Keep doing what I've been doing, I guess." Cree shrugged. "Only difference is..."

"Your feelings are more involved than before," Gramps added, completing his sentence.

Chuckling, Cree shook his head. *If he only knew,* he thought. He wasn't going to tell him how Leerah had kissed him. Some things needed to be kept only between them.

"They are, and you know I move from the heart, so it feels right but wrong at the same time."

"You know, all it took was one conversation for me and Minnie to take you in. Once we saw how your mama was moving out here, there wasn't anything else to discuss. We knew that had we allowed her to keep traveling with you or leaving you with other people; life would've given her a harsher reality check. We wouldn't have been able to live with that burden, so we took on one that we could."

"Damn." Cree chuckled. "I was a burden?"

"Damn right, you were. Not you necessarily, but the situation as a whole. We raised our kids, so starting all over took a lot of adjustment. We knew we couldn't screw up with you in our care because you already had two people who screwed you over."

Emotions bubbled in Cree's throat. Clearing it, he said, "I hope you know I appreciate you and Granny for everything."

"I know you do, son. Our decision was made so you could have the best life possible. We took on that role willingly, and I'm glad we did. Is that something you plan on doing with Leerah?"

"Possibly. As a friend, yes, I'm not sure about anything more right now."

"I'll tell you this, and you can do what you want with it. Don't start trying to fulfill a role in her or that child's life that you don't plan to keep. That's like planting a seed and never watering it but expecting it to grow. It can't because you didn't follow directions and nurture it. She's lost enough already. Make your intentions clear, you hear me?"

Cree nodded. "Yes, sir. I hear you."

"Good," Gramps said, standing from his lounge chair. "Come on out here to the garden and look at these tomatoes I been growing."

Cree stood as well, grinning. "Let me see what you been up to out here."

Some days were rough for Gramps around the house with his wife gone, but Cree was happy to see him still living. The sound advice he gave him came from a place of lessons Gramps had learned and from being happily married for over forty years. Keeping a family together was tough, but keeping a family together that didn't come from you was tougher. He hoped and prayed Cree was up for the challenge.

"HE'LL RESPECT WHATEVER CHOICE YOU MAKE."

SIX

"I'm trying really hard to protect my pussy and my peace," Leerah said randomly, catching Sovanna and Nae completely off guard.

Nae choked on the forkful of sweet potato noodles she'd just eaten. Patting her back, Sovanna looked at Leerah like she was crazy. During their girls' day outing, which consisted of shopping and pedicures, they stopped by Bibibop. The Asian fast-casual restaurant had become one of Leerah's favorite spots. She had to get that off her chest as soon as they sat in the booth. She'd been holding it in all day.

"Where did that come from?" Sovanna questioned.

"And who are you trying to protect them from?" Nae added.

While they waited for her answer, Leerah pondered how she'd explain what she meant without sounding crazier than she already had. Picking up her passionfruit lemonade, she took a generous swig.

"Y'all not gon' judge me are y'all?"

"Girl." Sovanna giggled. "We are the last ones to judge somebody."

Nae cleared her throat. "Exactly. I take my man back every other week."

"He must be your only nigga," Leerah cracked, making them laugh. Nae flicked her off. "No, but for real. I did something that I shouldn't have."

Curiously, Sovanna's eyes widened. "What?"

"I kissed Cree."

Nae's mouth dropped open while Sovanna smirked. Her lips pursed outwards in an "I told you" manner, making Leerah shake her head.

"See. There you go judging," Leerah groaned, eating some of her chicken and rice bowl.

"Shut the hell up. No, I'm not. I'm...shocked you're admitting there was something all along," Sovanna said.

"But there wasn't. I mean, not anymore. It's not like that. I think I was just in my feelings that day, and he came over and was just being so... I don't know, Cree. But better? Oh, my gosh. This is fucked up."

Nae snickered. She'd never seen her friend so flustered and nervous about a man.

"Did he kiss you back?" Sovanna asked.

Leerah squinted, thinking back to that night. She replayed the scene in her mind more than she'd like to admit.

"I mean, he didn't push me away."

"Aaah!" Nae's squeal of excitement made Leerah and Sovanna laugh. "I know that's right, Cree."

"He did step back, though," Leerah added. "Scolded me like a damn child."

"Because you know better." Sovanna snickered. "That was real bold of you, Ms. Ma'am."

"Real bold, but we love it. So, what happened next?" Nae wondered.

They were tuned in, hoping things had gone further, but Leerah had nothing more to give them, at least not about that night.

"Nothing. He left but doubled back to give me some money, and that's it. He's been texting and calling me, but I've been ignoring him," she said.

"Don't do him like that," Sovanna said.

"I want to do him, and that's the fucking problem," Leerah whined.

Sputtering laughter came from her two friends. Here they were trying to help her out, and she was being so unserious.

"Whoa. Okay, hold on. We went from nothing is going on between you two, to you kissing him, and now you want to fuck him?" Nae questioned, leaning in while asking.

"I'ma hoe, huh?" Leerah asked.

Sovanna couldn't help but cackle. "Please, shut up. You know how I feel about the situation," she said and shrugged.

Leerah looked to Nae for her answer.

"I mean...I'm not against it, but it is close to home. Like right on the damn doorstep. Nah, on the couch. You been to his house before?"

"Shut up, Nae." Sovanna giggled.

"I'm just asking!"

Huffing, Leerah rolled her eyes and continued eating. This was why she hadn't brought up the kiss to begin with. With the way Cree had been on her line and then stopped, leaving the ball in her court, she didn't know what to do. It wasn't like she could continue to ignore him. Doing so was eating her up inside. Then, he had the nerve to leave a voice note that Leerah replayed every time she thought of him. *You're sick*, she thought, frowning.

"Why you looking like that?" Nae asked.

"Was just thinking about the voice note he left me."

Sovanna grinned. "Ooh. Let us hear it. Wait. Was he talking freaky because I don't want to hear it if so?"

"Hell, I do. Cree looks like the type of nigga who talks you through it."

Leerah slid down in her seat. "Nae, pleeease. Don't even put that image in my head again."

"Again!" Sovanna screeched before lowering her voice. "See. Un, un. You've been holding out."

Pulling her phone out of her purse, Leerah went to her messages and pulled up their text thread. He hadn't sent another text, so the voice note sat there, daunting her. She typed and deleted so many messages in the last six days; it was comical. Mashing her finger into the up button to increase the volume, she pressed play. As soon as they heard him call her princess, both of their heads cocked to the side. A smirk teased the corners of Nae's mouth, while Sovanna's was in a full-blown smile.

"Yeeeah," Nae dragged. "He's definitely the talk

you through it type. I'm so sorry, friend. You gotta fuck him."

Leerah snorted. "You think so?"

"No! Don't do that. I mean, not yet," Sovanna urged. "I think it could be more than that."

"More than what?" Leerah asked.

"Something that's only driven by lust. You're probably not going to like what I have to say about this, but I'm going to say it anyway. That's why we're best friends," Sovanna said.

A decade-plus of friendship gave them the comfort to express themselves freely. They weren't each other's yes men and didn't always agree on things, but that was the nature of having mature relationships. Friends who love and care about you want to see you at your best and lift you up at your lowest. Those tough conversations were meant to be had, and Leerah was all ears.

"I'm listening," she said.

Reaching across the table, she grabbed Leerah's hand. "You're grieving," Sovanna said plainly. Gently. She spoke with love, and liquid gathered in Leerah's eyes. "There's no right or wrong way to grieve. You have to be willing to understand that some decisions you make are because of that. I don't want your confusion to ruin a good thing between you and Cree."

"But I'm not confused," Leerah sniveled.

"Okay, maybe not, and if that's the case, why have you been ignoring him?"

She didn't have an answer because she wasn't ready to admit to herself that whatever was happening between them, when she let it, was something she wasn't prepared for. Not mentally, at least.

"He's a lot in a good way, and I know he means well. But then there's me trying to make it something it shouldn't be."

"But you don't know what it could be if you don't let things just flow," Nae said.

Leerah wiped her tears that stubbornly fell. "Grieving is so annoying. I'm really heartbroken that Terrance is gone, but not for me, you know? Moreso for Landon. And I feel bad because I want to move on and enjoy my life, but in the back of my mind, I can't because the person who was a huge part of the life I'm living now is gone. Terrance should've been the one putting our baby's toys together that night, y'all. Not Cree."

Sovanna blinked rapidly, keeping her tears at bay. Nae wasn't a crier, but her chest ached seeing her friend so torn.

"But it was him, and you didn't have to ask him, Leerah," Sovanna said. "He came through for you and always has."

"So, what're you saying? Because you're confusing me. One minute, you're telling me to see where things with him could go, and the next, it's slow down because I'm grieving. Make up your mind, hoe."

Sovanna chuckled. "Tell yourself that. But what I'm saying is that it's okay for you to move on when you feel like you're ready. Hell, even when you're not, but be careful. Don't let lust cloud your mind, but also don't let the fear of the future stop you from pursuing more. Cree isn't just some random man we're talking about. He's your friend before anything, and if I know him like I think I do, he'll respect whatever choice you make."

And that's exactly why Leerah was confused and wanted to slowly drag her pussy across Cree's handsome face like a snail. He was such a fucking man and made her feel so much at ease. In his presence, Leerah felt so soft and shy but still able to be her true self with him. It had her questioning what she shared with Terrance and whether it came remotely close to what she felt now.

"Yeah." Leerah sighed. "I know he will. I

don't want to lead him on either or look stupid if I try to kiss him again. That man's lips…" All she could do was shake her head. "I know Terrance is rolling over in his grave, ready to beat my ass."

Sovanna gasped loudly. "Leerah!"

"Why the fuck would you say that?" Nae cackled, unable to hold back her laughter.

Leerah shrugged. "What? He probably is. I can hear him now. *Damn, Leerah. My godbrother? You a cold piece of work, shawty. You been wanting to fuck with that nigga, huh*?" she said, deepening her voice to mimic him.

Sovanna wanted to laugh so badly, but she didn't feel it was appropriate. "I'm not even about to go there with you. Grow up."

"If anything, you need to be asking that man for a sign to give you his blessing," Nae suggested.

"That'll never happen. Plus, who says Cree wants to even be on that with me?" Leerah asked.

"From the sounds of that voice message and what you've been telling me, he's been waiting for you to make a move," Sovanna said.

"Didn't he introduce you to Terrance?" Nae asked.

Leerah nodded. "Yeah."

"Shit, I wouldn't be surprised if he had a thing for you all this time and just kept it hidden."

Tending to the remainder of her food, Nae didn't catch the stunned look in Leerah's eyes, but Sovanna did. She also saw the way she rubbed at her neck. It was a tic of hers that led Sovanna to believe that there was much more she wasn't telling.

"Well, there's only one way to find out," Sovanna announced, smiling.

"Nope. I don't even want to hear a suggestion." Leerah shook her head.

Sovanna's head tilted backward as she laughed. "Why not? Aren't you the same person who encouraged me to go on a date with Zahir? Now, look at us. Happily, in a relationship."

"That's different. Y'all already had some foundation built between y'all."

"And you and Cree don't? Please be so for real right now, Leerah," Nae said, sucking her teeth. "If you a scary hoe, then just say that."

"I ain't scared of a mothafuckin' thing," Leerah sassed, rolling her neck with tooted-out lips. She dared Nae to call her bluff, and she did just that.

"Okay, bet. So, we're pulling up on Cree when we leave here."

Nae wasn't asking a question.

"And you know where he's at how?" Leerah asked.

"See. Look at you. Don't be using that voice with me like I'm keeping tabs on your nigga." Nae laughed. "But I just saw a picture of him and Saleem with his fine ass."

"He's very much so married," Sovanna said.

"Oh. He is?"

Nae sounded as if Saleem wasn't, and that rubbed Sovanna and Leerah the wrong way. They were cool with his wife, Amira, and they were still together, to their knowledge.

"You know something we don't?" Leerah asked.

"Nope. Nothing enough to prove he isn't married. Plus, that's not my business to tell."

Sovanna grunted. "Should've never brought it up. Now I'm curious. I'm glad we're going to see Cree. We can stop at Saleem's store while we're there."

"And this one girl's store I follow on Instagram. She just opened a new athletic clothing store inside the strip," Nae added, scooting out of the booth.

Sovanna scootched out behind her while Leerah stayed seated. In her mind, she could face Cree like a big girl and tell him what she'd been thinking. Following through with it was a completely different task, and she hoped she didn't end up looking like a fool by the end of the day.

"I had no idea they were making workout clothes this cute," Nae said, holding the mulberry-colored dress to her body.

Leerah glanced her way and had to agree. The color looked good against Nae's caramel skin tone. She held a sky-blue short set that she planned on purchasing. Curve Me wasn't just a store that had apparel. It had a variety of products tailored to athletes and people on a fitness journey. Some of the equipment included resistant bands, dumbbells, foam rollers, and yoga mats. Leerah loved the accessories tailored for women. She hadn't worked out in ages but being in here motivated her to at least get back to walking. Since having Landon, she hadn't worked out at all, but her body was still nice in her eyes. He'd given her an extra thickness that Leerah wanted to keep.

"Yes, that's real cute. I think I'ma get this set and a white dress. Sovanna, what you getting?"

Sovanna swiveled away from the men's section. "Wouldn't this be cute for me and Zahir?" She held a black and white, his and hers set out to show them.

"You can't help yourself." Leerah chuckled. "But yes. I like that."

"Y'all finding everything okay?" the owner of the store asked, coming from the back.

Leerah smiled, loving her stylish get-up. She was rocking hot pink leggings and a cropped set that enhanced her curvy frame. An array of colorful waist beads circled her thick waist. The definition in her arms and the glow of her skin let Leerah know that she was a frequent member of the gym.

"Hey. Yes, we are. Are you the owner?" Leerah asked.

"I am," she said, grinning. "I'm Danielle, but everyone calls me Dani."

"It's nice to meet you, Dani girl. Your store is really nice. I'ma have to bring my mama in here," Nae said.

Dani's face lit up. "I'd love that. This is my first storefront, so I'd love the support."

"Oh. You have ours. How long have you been in business?" Sovanna asked.

"A little over four years now. I started in the basement of my aunt's house, and the business kept growing, so I had to grow with it," Dani explained.

Leerah clapped. "I know that's right. Congratulations! And the name is so cute and catchy. What made you choose Curve Me?"

"Thank you," Dani said and chuckled. "It's kind of a funny, glow-up, get-back story. An ex of mine cheated on me and claimed it wasn't working out because I was too fat. He didn't know I had a few health issues that caused significant weight gain, but whatever. I started working out with a personal trainer, hired a nutritionist, and put my all into my brand. About a year after he ended things, I saw him out, and he tried hollering at me."

"Hell no! Just like a bum ass man," Nae sneered.

"Right," Dani agreed. "Of course, I brushed him off, and he was like, damn, you gon' curve me like that? And I said, didn't you curve me when you thought I was too big?"

"Okay!"

"I know that's right!"

The girls hooted and hollered, cheering for Dani's glow-up and clapback.

"So, that's where it came from. I knew as soon as he walked away what I'd change the name to, and it stuck," Dani said. "Plus, I believe women and men should embrace their curves no matter their size. But also take their health seriously. That's the mission here. To embrace your curves healthily and look good while doing so."

"Oh, girl. You're going to be getting all my little money," Nae said. "Hold on. And you have workout plans?" She picked up a pamphlet from one of the tables and scanned it over.

"Yes. My fiancé, who is still my personal trainer, designs them." Dani smiled widely as she watched Leerah and Sovanna grab a pamphlet. This was what made her days.

"I'ma keep this for the future. Let me get out of this store before I buy everything up." Leerah chuckled while picking up a water bottle.

"I won't complain about that," Dani said as she walked around to the register to help her employee check them out.

Before they left, they made sure they were following her on Instagram and wished her and her business well. Leerah hadn't planned on spending any more money for the day, but she was all for supporting Black businesses, especially when they were Black women-owned.

"Y'all better not fake on me when it's time to work out," Nae said as they walked the hall.

Leerah snickered. "I'm not going to even lie to you; I'ma need a notice a few days in advance if we're going to the gym. I have to get my mind right. Can we start off light, like walking? Why do you want to go straight into being a bodybuilder?"

They laughed loudly, catching a few glances from patrons walking by. Something about Black people laughing loudly, unashamed of their happiness, made people tune in. Everyone wanted to know what they had to smile and be happy about. It was the small things like cracking jokes with your friends about working out, knowing one of y'all was faking.

Nae stopped walking. "See. I didn't even say all that. Being in the gym may motivate you more because you'll be around other people. My skinny self needs to do some weightlifting. Look at my arms."

Even after having her daughter, Nae only weighed a good one hundred and twenty-one pounds. Nothing was wrong with that; her high metabolism made it harder for her to gain weight.

"What's wrong with them?" Leerah asked.

"They're so little. My legs, too. Just skinny and no meat."

Sovanna shrugged. "So, what? Do you think

you're too skinny, or has the image of what society deemed a woman's body should look like gotten to your head?"

Nae twisted her lips, thinking. She'd always been on the smaller side and thought she'd at least put on some grown woman weight everyone talked about in their mid-thirties. When that didn't happen, and her weight didn't peak once she had her daughter, she began critiquing herself much more.

"Both. Hell, I want some ass like Leerah," Nae said, playfully smacking her on the booty.

"Girl, no, you don't. Imagine getting a nice pair of jeans over your thighs, only for them not to fit over your behind. The shit is so annoying. Plus, you know what they say. What you lack in the back—"

"You pack in the cat!" Sovanna and Nae completed her sentence, cracking up. Nae patted between her legs and thrusted her hips.

"Okay, Evelyn." Leerah laughed, calling her the woman from a reality TV show.

"Y'all are too funny. Oh, look. Saleem is at work and look who he's talking to," Sovanna said.

So engrossed in their conversation, Leerah didn't realize they made it to the other end of the strip until now. The family-friendly tunes playing in the hallway vanished once they crossed the threshold of

Jennie Mae's Juicery. The name was an ode to Saleem's late grandmother. Larry June's *Organic Smiles* bumped through the speakers, making the women smoothly bob their heads. A few customers were sitting down while some were in line.

Leerah noticed none of them, only the man who'd been invading her every thought since she tasted his lips. Time didn't slow down as she took Cree in; it sped up. She took in his every feature, loving the business casual look he'd gone with for the day. His relaxed gray pants and lightweight mauve MAG Co. collar button-down looked so good against his cocoa skin. She caught a glimpse of a gold rope chain hanging from his neck while a Talley and Twine watch was clasped around his left wrist.

Leerah wanted to keep admiring him, but Cree had other plans. His gaze fastened on her as she tried to act like she hadn't just been staring him down. While she looked away, greeting Saleem with a hug, Cree let his eyes roam freely. Not having seen her in over a week made him appreciate her absence. He caught a few men sitting around looking her way and smirked. Leerah garnered attention without effort, and Cree wondered if she knew how attractive that was.

When her eyes did land on him again, Cree nodded upward and licked his lips. "The princess decided to grace me with her presence."

He would've seen the blush on her cheeks if she had a lighter complexion. "Not intentionally. The girls wanted to grab a juice."

"Yeah?" he questioned, deciding not to call her bluff. "That's what's up. You look good."

She paired some mid-thigh denim shorts with a multi-colored crochet top and Prada crochet sandals. Her wash-and-go black curls were parted down the middle and draped down her back. Cree fingered the hem of her top, urging her to come closer to him.

"So do you. Thank you."

"You made this?" he asked.

Leerah nodded. "Yes."

He knew she liked to crochet in her spare time and had even accumulated a few items she made for him.

"I like it."

"Thank you. You're just with all the compliments today, huh?" she jested, making him chuckle.

"You can get them any day, every day. It's nothing."

She pursed her lips, cutely smirking. "Mhm. Tell me anything."

Cree focused on her pretty, questioning brown eyes. He had a few things he wanted to get off his chest. Leaning down, he positioned his lips near her ear while rubbing a hand across her exposed midsection.

"Come here. Let me talk to you real quick," he said, then walked toward the back of the store where the tables were unoccupied.

Leerah blew out a deep breath and followed him. She should've known coming here was a bad idea. His touch and intoxicating scent had her ready to spill her heart out. Cree stood near the extended counter, giving her the space to stand in front of him so he could watch their surroundings.

"Why do I feel like I just got called into the principal's office?" Leerah giggled.

Cree smirked. "Because you did. I ain't gon' ask you the obvious, so what's up? What Lando been up to?"

"Nothing. Enjoying his toys and driving me crazy."

"Them toys I put together, huh? I should go and disassemble them. Make you put 'em together on your own."

Leerah laughed. "That's so wrong. Don't do that."

"Nah. I wouldn't do that. But you had a few more

days of ignoring me before I showed you what I'm really 'bout."

Leerah's clit thumped. She loved getting a nigga riled up, but this was on a different level. Cree was giving out foreplay without touching her. A man good with his words surely had to be better with his mouth, and Leerah wanted to test her theory.

"You're talking crazy," Leerah said, loving every bit of how he was talking.

Tell me more! Tell me more! she chanted in her head.

"I'm keeping it real with you. What's on your mind? Talk to me."

Cree placed his hands inside his pockets and leaned against the counter. He was chewing on a piece of minty gum, flexing that scrumptious jaw of his. Leerah could hardly focus. His full lips, like always, were moisturized and teasing her worse than before.

I just want to drag my tongue all over them, she thought and chuckled.

"C'mon, goofy girl. Stop staring and talk to me. We can't keep acting like you ain't put your lips on me."

Smacking his chest, Leerah laughed. "See. Here I was trying to forget it even happened."

"Again?" he questioned, head cocked to the side.

They shared a known look. Secrets passed between them shifted the energy in the room. Leerah despised and hated it when he looked at her how he was now. It was as if he urged her to admit more than she wanted to but still had enough respect for her to let her keep getting away with not doing so. And he did.

"Yes." Leerah sighed.

"My thing is this... why would you give me a sample *again* if I'm not allowed to indulge fully?"

Leerah stopped breathing. *Lord, this man.* She squeezed her eyes shut and wished she could cross her legs. "Cree, please."

"I'm listening, Princess."

Leerah peeled her eyes open. "I shouldn't have kissed you. Yes, I wanted to, and that's me being completely honest, but I know it's wrong. I was deadass wrong. You and I both know it."

"Okay. You were wrong, but how did you feel? That shit didn't feel right?" Cree asked, removing a hand from his pocket.

Leerah's eyes ventured there, and she hated that they did. The imprint of his dick made her mouth water. It stood out thickly against his slim leg, and it took all the willpower she could muster up not to caress him.

"It felt like I was betraying my baby daddy," Leerah finally answered.

Cree nodded. "A'ight. Respect. Besides that, what was going through your mind? You don't just kiss a nigga with no explanation, then ignore him like he was in the wrong."

"Why do we have to talk about this?" she whined.

Grabbing her around the waist, Cree pulled her into him. Leerah's breath hitched at their close contact. His dick, which was so fucking hard, was pressed against her soft stomach. She looked at him with wide eyes.

"Just stand right here for a second," Cree said lowly, needing his erection to go away. He thought pulling her into him to hide it would help, but her powdery scent, soft body, and teasing lips only made it worse.

"People might be looking at us," Leerah whispered. Her heart was beating so fast.

"And I only have eyes for you. So, answer my question, and I'll let you go."

Leera tilted her head back, trying to gather her thoughts. It was difficult when he held her like this, talked like he knew exactly what he wanted from her, and was ready to risk it all. They were caked up in the middle of their friend's store as if no one could see them, and Cree didn't care. Boldly, he was letting her know what it was and needed to ensure she was on the same page before flipping to the next one. He just knew their story didn't end like this again.

Exhaling, Leerah said, "I already told you I wanted to kiss you. I don't know why; I just did. I make love to you, I want to be with you, but I fuck with other females occasionally. That's the situation. You feel better now? That's some honesty for yo' ass."

Cree's boisterous laugh brought tears to his eyes. Leerah held hers in, watching his Adam's apple bob and white teeth sparkle. It was so infectious that she couldn't help but giggle. He needed that laugh to help ease some of the scalding tension between them.

"Man," he muttered, still laughing. "You shot out for that. This ain't no Baby Boy scene."

"No?" Leerah teased, grinning.

Cree shook his head. "Never. That nigga Jody was a bum. He wasn't man enough to take care of his family and cherish the woman he had. That'll never be me, and I'd never put you in that position."

Leerah sobered at his words. "I know you wouldn't, and that's what scares me the most."

Clearing his throat, Cree said, "I get that. There's a ton of reasons for you to be scared but let me show you why you shouldn't be. Can I do that?"

Going with her gut and listening to the beat of her tender heart, Leerah nodded. "As friends!" she blurted, then lowered her voice. "For now. Can we ... test the waters first?"

His gaze softened. "Of course, Princess. I'm a great swimmer. How deep can I go?"

Leerah's nipples swelled at his question. Cree wasn't playing fair and wouldn't from this day forward. She'd given him the green light, and all bets were off. Leerah would've led him straight to the deep end if she hadn't wanted to take things slowly. She was so turned on, she thought about stepping inside the walk-in refrigerator to cool off.

"Just stick your t—"

Cree's brows dented. "My what?"

"Your toe!" Leerah screeched. "I was going to say your toe, but you cut me off."

"Oh. A'ight. I was just checking." Cree laughed, loosening his hold on her. "Stick my toe in, see what the temperature is like. Got it. Anything else?"

She shook her head. "No. My goodness." Leerah laughed, rubbing her neck.

"Good. Come taste this new juice mix on the menu. You need to cool off."

Again, Leerah followed behind him. At this point, she wasn't sure if it was because Cree was an amazing leader or if he had some type of spell on her. Either way, she was following his lead. His assurance excited her to see where things with them could go, but she knew it would come with some backlash she wasn't prepared for.

SEVEN

Leerah knew she should've gone with her first mind and stayed home.

Having a close relationship with Terrance's family had its ups and downs; right now, it was the downside. Andrea invited her over to celebrate Terrance's grandmother's birthday. Leerah was happy to give Mrs. Jackie her flowers and let Landon enjoy his family, but now she wondered if she had only been invited to get berated.

As soon as she entered the kitchen where a few aunties and cousins were, whatever conversation they were having ceased. All eyes landed on Leerah, letting it be known that she was the topic of the conversation. Kenia was the only one who said something, breaking the awkward silence.

"You came to get another plate, girl?" she asked cheerily.

Leerah saw right through her façade. "Something to drink. What's up? Y'all didn't have to stop talking once I entered the room."

"We weren't talking about anything important," Kenia said.

At the round wooden table, Vee grunted like that was a lie. Leerah wasn't going to say anything at first, but how a few of their expressions changed made her eager to figure out what was up.

"What was that, Ms. Vee?" Leerah questioned.

"Y'all. Please don't start," Kenia pleaded.

Vee swirled the wine in her glass and took a sip. It was her second of the evening, and she was already feeling it. "I ain't say nothing, child."

"Yeah, okay. Everybody gets hush-hush when I enter the room." Leerah chuckled. "If y'all need to get something off y'all chest, say that."

"I mean, she does have a point," one of the cousins, Olivia, said. Leerah liked her, and they had kicked it together a few times.

Leerah glanced her way before looking around the kitchen. Everyone was quiet until one cousin, whom Leerah couldn't recall ever meeting, grabbed her attention.

"We just think it's weird that you've moved on from our cousin already."

Looking her over, Leerah took in her neat box braids and baby doll face. She looked young but old enough to get checked.

"And do you know me?" Leerah questioned.

"I know enough about you to know that my cousin wouldn't approve of what you been doing."

Leerah chuckled as they all stared at her. "Little girl, whoever the hell you are, you don't know a thing about me besides my name. And you probably only know that because it stays in y'all mouth."

"My name is Stasia, and I ain't no little girl," she sassed, snaking her neck. "Kenia, you better let her know what's up with me."

"Nah. You let me know what's up." Leerah smiled, hoping she stood up.

Kenia pulled Leerah back some even though she hadn't made a move. But she knew her. She'd seen her fight more than a few times, and Stasia wasn't ready to get embarrassed.

"Now, we ain't about to do all that in here," one of the aunties said. "Leerah, honey. All we were saying was that maybe you should wait on dating."

"Especially if it's Cree," Vee said, dropping his name with a smirk.

Having an idea of why they'd been discussing her, Leerah wasn't surprised that Cree's name was brought up. Vee was messy like that and clearly hadn't gotten over him paying up Landon's daycare, but why was she still the topic? Why was anything regarding her financial status and son being brought up? It made no sense and aggravated her to no end.

"Vee," she said, dropping all signs of respect. "I could've sworn we had a conversation about you being in my business," Leerah said.

"Vee? Oh, honey, don't get beside yourself. I'm Ms. Vee, to you."

"You're my baby daddy's auntie; let's get that clear," Leerah clarified. "Why is my relationship status or who I'm dating any of y'all's concern?"

"Ask Kenia. She's the one who saw y'all hugged up," Stasia said, throwing her under the bus.

Gawking at her cousin, Kenia couldn't hide the guilt on her face when Leerah's head swiveled her way.

"Leerah, you know it's not like that," Kenia said, ready to plead her case.

"Then, what is it like because if you had an issue, though I wouldn't care, you could've said something to me. Instead, like always, you resort to being messy like your miserable ass mama."

"Apple didn't fall too far from the tree," someone said with a giggle.

Leerah shook her head as Kenia frowned. "Nah. The apple didn't fall off the tree at all. It just turned rotten."

Stasia stood up from her chair. "You better watch your mouth."

"Or what? Who gon' check me?" Leerah questioned.

It was apparent no one was, but they were faking like they would. Murmurs and whispers floated around the space, making her roll her eyes.

"You out of pocket for that, Leerah."

"Damn, Cree?" someone whispered.

"Auntie Vee is messy, though. Kenia, too."

"So, what? She been single," Olivia defended her.

Vee and some other people stood up from the table. Leerah looked at them, waiting for someone to jump crazy, just as Andrea walked into the kitchen.

"What's going on in here?" she asked, looking at everyone with scowls on their faces. Andrea focused on Leerah, who seemed to be the only calm one.

"Leerah about to get her ass whooped for talking to me crazy," Vee said.

Laughing loudly, Leerah said, "Get my ass

whooped by who? Not by you or this little girl. Walk up on me if you want to. I'ma drag you all around this kitchen," she promised when Stasia stepped her way.

Kenia pulled her back, but Leerah jerked out of her grasp, giving her an icy glare. "Don't touch me."

"Hold on, now. Ain't nobody putting hands on anybody in my house. Leerah, what's the problem?" Andrea questioned.

"Obviously, it's me, so I'ma remove myself and Landon from the picture," Leerah hissed.

Vee sucked her teeth. "See. What I tell you. As soon as something didn't go her way, she would keep Landon from us."

"I'm not about to sit up here and have my son around people who don't like me! It's not about getting my way; it's about minding your fucking business!" Leerah fumed.

"And you think messing around with Cree is okay? He's family!" Vee shouted, making more people nosily venture toward the kitchen.

Andrea frowned, not believing what she just heard. "What?"

"Mhm. Kenia saw them all booed up at the mall. Just trifling," Vee said with disgust.

"You got one more time, and I'ma knock that

ugly ass toupee off your head, and I put that on your nephew."

Andrea lightly shoved Leerah back. "No. You're not knocking anything off anyone's head, especially from my sisters. Cut this mess out. Vee, you shut your messy ass up. All in this girl's business. I'm sick of y'all coming over here causing drama. We're here to celebrate my mama, and y'all starting mess."

"But Auntie, she's in the wrong. Why would she mess with Cree, of all people?" Stasia said, a bratty whine laced through her words. If Leerah didn't know better, she'd think the girl wanted Cree for herself.

"Girl, shut up. 'cause wasn't you just smashing your quote-unquote best friends, man?" Olivia asked, already knowing the answer.

The two cousins had a stare-off but didn't say anything else. Andrea shook her head. This was too much.

"I'm not about to let y'all sit up here and gang up on Leerah because y'all have an issue with how she's living her life. My son would want her to do what's best for her and Landon. As family, I thought y'all would to. Now, if y'all can't be cordial and act like y'all got some sense, everyone can leave," Andrea advised.

"Oh. I was leaving anyway. I'm sorry for disrespecting your house, Mrs. Andrea, but I know when I'm not welcome somewhere. And Vee, that daycare fee you like to keep mentioning, consider it a parting gift. Landon will not be going there anymore," Leerah said, making everyone gasp.

Vee's mouth opened and then closed. Stuck on stupid, she had nothing else to say.

"See what you did, Mama!" Kenia cried.

"No, you did that by running your mouth. Leerah hasn't done anything to you," Olivia fussed. She sometimes picked up shifts at the daycare and now wouldn't get to see Landon.

Leerah didn't care whose feelings were hurt, but it damn sure wouldn't be her son's. Andrea followed her out of the kitchen and to the backyard, where Landon played with the other kids.

"What up, Leerah. You been doing okay?" one of Terrance's uncles asked.

"Hey, Bone. I've been good. About to get this little boy so we can go."

Sighing heavily, Andrea stopped at the top of the patio steps, watching her descend them. Leerah walked over to the two-story playset Andrea bought just for Landon and Tink and waited for them to come down the slide.

"Yay!" Tink cheered, slapping her hands. "We did it, brother."

Landon clapped his hands and took off running but stopped when he saw his mama. All traces of how angry she was moments before now dissipated. She smiled at him while running a hand through his chunky two-strand twists. Though she had no plans of locking his hair when Cree asked, she wondered how he would look with them, and he was adorable —running around looking like a mini-Terrance.

"Come on, baby. It's time to go."

Tink ran over to them with her braided ponytail swinging. "Y'all leaving?"

"Yes," Leerah answered.

"Aww, man. It's like he just got here. Can I come with y'all?" Tink asked.

"Not today, baby. Maybe next week," Leerah said, tying the shoestring on his Nike Dunks.

She grabbed Landon's hand and tried walking away, but he fell out. Tink's bottom lip poked out, seeing him cry.

"He doesn't want to leave me," she said.

Leerah felt bad, but she wasn't in the mood. Swooping him up, she placed Landon on her hip. "He doesn't have a choice. I'll have him call your iPad later."

"Okay. Give me a hug, brother," she cooed.

Leerah lowered him to her height so they could hug. Tink quickly kissed his cheek and took off to go play. Once she made it up the patio, Leerah gave a general goodbye to everyone. They were trying to ask her questions and get Landon to stay, but she wasn't having it. Andrea followed her inside the house, where Leerah wished Mrs. Jackie happy birthday again and let her love on Landon before heading out the front door.

"Y'all don't have to leave, but I know your mind is made up," Andrea said, stopping at the back passenger door.

Leerah placed Landon in his car seat and searched for his pacifier. She did not want to hear all the crying on the ride home.

"It is. If I stay, someone is getting beat up, and Mrs. Jackie deserves to enjoy her day," Leerah said, placing the binky in Landon's mouth.

He sniffled and quieted immediately. His light brown wet eyes made her chest cave with regret, but Leerah knew she had to go.

"I hate that things have even come to this," Andrea said.

"It's not your fault. People can't mind their business. I still love you, and you can get Landon whenever you want. That sister and niece of yours, though? Absolutely not."

She didn't care that she had to search for a new daycare. For the sake of her sanity, Leerah wouldn't dare have her baby surrounded by people with evil intentions.

"I don't know what their issue is, but they better get it together. You are always welcome in my home, and you know that," Andrea reassured, taking hold of her hand.

Leerah squeezed it. "I know, and I appreciate everything you do for me and Landon. But I can't be around people who make me feel like it's wrong to live my life and talk about me behind my back."

"I understand one hundred percent. You have to do what's best for you and Landon. Just don't make me pay for it," Andrea said, smiling.

Leerah weakly smiled back. "I won't."

"Good. Text me when y'all make it home."

She told her okay and climbed into the driver's seat. Leerah wasn't two minutes into her drive before she broke down crying. Her tears were of frustration and hurt more than sadness. It angered her that people felt entitled to speak on her life. Until they lost the father of their child, they needed to shut the hell up.

When she came to a red light, Leerah navigated the dashboard screen to call her mama. Katrina picked up on the second ring.

"Hey, hey," she said sweetly.

"Mama," Leerah cried, choking on the word.

Katrina immediately sat up on the couch, panic surging through her. "What's the matter? Are you and Landon okay?"

Leerah's chest stuttered. "Can...Can we come over there? I'm so pissed off right now; I'm shaking."

"Where are you at? Do you think you can drive? Baby, find my keys for me," she said, talking to her husband, Keith.

"Yes, I can drive," Leerah sniffled. "We're leaving Ms. Andrea's house. I had to get up out of there before I caught a charge."

"For what? Hold on, let me find my shoes," she said, placing her on speaker. "Go 'head, I'm listening."

"I got into it with Ms. Vee, and she started talking crazy to me. I guess one of Terrance's cousins saw me and Cree hugged up the other day, and now everybody has something to say."

"So fucking what! Is this their life, or is it yours? And you know what? I've been letting Vee slide since you told me about her years ago, but she got the right one today."

"Babe, chill out. Lee-Lee, you headed this way, baby girl?" Keith asked.

"Yes. About ten minutes away."

"All right. We'll be here. You got your mama tying up her sneakers and shit." Keith chuckled, making Leerah grin.

Katrina sucked her teeth. "That lady ain't about to keep playing with my child or my grandbaby. Why is she so concerned about what Leerah has going on when her nephew had some whole other chick in the car when he passed away? She better stop playing with me."

"All right, Trina." Keith placated her. "Leerah is still on the phone."

"I know that. She and I have talked about this before. For one, they weren't together. So, what she does and with whom is her business. I can guarantee that none of them over there, besides Andrea, has done half as much as Cree since Terrance has been gone. I'll bet you this fifty-dollar bill in my pocket right now," Katrina insisted.

Leerah cleared her throat. "They haven't, and that's what has me so pissed off. He was living his life and lying to me. So, does that mean I have to be lonely because he's gone? I deserve to be happy too, Mama." Her voice cracked, and more tears fell.

Katrina simmered down and sat on the bed. "You do, baby. And you'll get every bit of happiness this world has to offer. If that just so happens to be Cree who makes you happy, then that's just what it is. Fuck Vee and anyone else who has something to say about it."

Silence drifted through the line as Leerah sniffled and wiped her face. She told her mama almost everything, so she already knew about her and Cree. Katrina had given her motherly advice, but that was it. She didn't bash her for what they could grow to be or even judge her. If she hadn't, Katrina didn't know why Vee or anyone else thought they could.

Leerah was so thankful for her parents, especially her mama. Being able to call her when she needed a listening ear, a shoulder to cry on, or an ear to cackle loudly in, wasn't something she took for granted. Some days, that's all she needed. She knew she could count on her mama if she didn't have anyone else's support. Katrina's love outweighed all the hate everyone seemingly now had for her daughter.

"She still rocking those Chewbacca wigs?" Keith asked.

Leerah laughed and wished they were on Face-Time so she could see her mama's face. Only her daddy could take a serious moment and make a joke, but she appreciated it, and he knew it.

Giggling, she said, "Yes, and was about to get it snatched right off her head, too."

"We gon' catch her slipping one of these days," Keith joked.

"We sure will, and you gon' have to bail me out of jail," Katrina added. "You sure you don't need us to meet you?"

Leerah came to a stop sign down the street from their house and glanced in the backseat. Landon stared back at her, melting Leerah's heart. For her baby, she would go to war with whoever, whenever.

"I'm sure. We're down the street."

"Okay. We'll see y'all in a little bit then," Katrina said.

Leerah hung up. She inhaled, licked her lips, and shifted her foot off the brake. The movement symbolized her life. It'd been placed on hold to be with Terrance, waiting for him to get his life together and prove her wrong, but she could no longer remain stagnant. If she didn't give her life some gas, she'd remain stuck, unhappy, and continuously grieving what didn't work out.

That was no way to live, and though she missed him, had missed him before he even passed, somebody was waiting and ready to fill the void. She knew what people were thinking, probably calling her all kinds of names except the one on her birth certificate, but Leerah didn't care.

Cree wasn't a rebound; he was a reward.

Leerah deserved every uplifting word, sense of security, outpouring of love, unwavering support, and utmost respect he had to give. If it came with some dick on the side, she could have that, too, if she wanted it, and that was no one's business but theirs.

"I GOT EVERYTHING I NEED RIGHT NEXT TO ME."

EIGHT

A night out on the town was exactly what Leerah needed. When Nae hit her up, wanting to check out a new hookah lounge, she readily accepted the invite. Then, she called Sovanna so she could go as well. At thirty-two, Leerah had partied and clubbed enough to enjoy only being on the scene a few days out of the month. If she was, it was a laidback spot like Elite where the vibes were grown and the crowd behaved.

When they arrived, Nae told them it was an exclusive, members-only hookah lounge that was invite-only. Depending on the invitee, determined the number of guests you could bring with you, then you could sign up to become one. Nae invited them and her sister, Toni. Leerah loved that it wasn't too bougie, the drinks were good and strong, the DJ was spinning straight jams, and the patrons were enjoying themselves.

Leerah snapped her fingers and swayed sensually to the sounds of *Bae* by Skilla Baby. Cutely, she blew smoke from her gold mouth tip. The peach-watermelon flavor wasn't overpowering, and it tasted good, but she still had to adjust to it with each pull. She was used to puffing on her tobacco and nicotine-free hookah pens from Blakk Smoke.

"This your song, friend?" Sovanna asked, smirking.

"Mhm. You know I'm a bad bitch. Classy nails, French tip," she rapped, wiggling her French tip nails that matched her toes.

Leerah kept it cute and simple for the evening, wearing a short-sleeved denim dress that cinched at the waist and silver high-heel sandals. She'd been receiving compliments from men and women all night. Switching her hairstyle up, she flat ironed her curls but kept her signature part down the middle.

"Anybody want another drink?" Toni asked.

Leerah nodded while Sovanna and Nae declined for now. They had a few shots in the car before they came in and were mellow.

"Yeah. I'll come with you to the bar," Leerah said, standing up.

She tugged her dress down and grabbed her purse off the faux leather bench. Following Toni's short frame, Leerah admired her waist-length sandy brown sister locs. Thanks to her mama, she'd been growing them since she was a preteen, and she loved them.

"Y'all looking real good tonight, ladies," a handsome man complimented as they approached the bar.

He stood beside Leerah, adjusting the heavy chain around his neck. She looked him over, surmising that he wasn't her type without much thought. Still, she thanked him because she wasn't rude.

"Thank you."

"What you drinking on tonight?" he asked.

She eyed the drink menu, faking like she had no clue. "Haven't decided yet."

"A'ight. When you do, it's on me."

"The drinks come with the membership, sweetie," Toni leaned over and said.

A wave of embarrassment washed over him. Chuckling, he played it off. "Damn. I didn't know that. This my first time here," he offered. "Good looking out."

Toni smiled. "No problem."

A bartender approached, ready to take their orders. "Hi. What can I get for you?" she asked.

"May I have a Sidecar, please? What you getting?" she asked Leerah, who was trying to give ol' boy a hint that she wasn't interested.

"I'll take a French 75," she said.

"Got it. I'll have those right over for you."

Toni responded to a text message while Leerah waited for her bar buddy to stop standing beside her. She thought facing away from him would let him know she would pass, but instead, it made him introduce himself.

"I'm Mark," he said, holding his hand out for her to shake.

Leerah gave him a forced smile. "Nice to meet you."

"Damn. I can't get your name?" He chuckled.

"I'm just here to enjoy my night. Not give out my name that surely doesn't come with a number."

Taken aback by her straightforwardness, Mark wanted her even more. He wasn't the type that couldn't take being rejected, though.

Nodding, he said, "You got it, beautiful. Enjoy your night."

"You do the same," Leerah said.

Mark walked off, and Leerah released a sigh.

"You could've given that man your name." Toni tittered.

"Girl, hell no. I couldn't tell at first, but that was not his hair. It looked like he glued one of those curly 27-piece wigs on from back in the day, cut it down, and sprayed it with hair dye."

Toni tossed a hand over her mouth, masking her laugh. "Shut up. He did not."

"I promise you. I don't know what it is with people and their horrible wigs, girl. They gotta get it together." Leerah chuckled.

She was mainly talking about Vee, who had apparently sobered up this morning and texted her phone. Leerah wasn't accepting half-ass apologies when the disrespect was as loud as the crowd at a Chiefs game home opener. Plus, a drunk mind would forever reveal sober thoughts. Leerah wanted Vee, Kenia, and whoever else had a problem with her to stand ten toes on not liking her because she wasn't budging.

The bar was somewhat packed, and there were only two bartenders, so they hadn't received their drinks yet. Going inside her purse, Leerah pulled out some cash to leave as a tip. While Toni conversed with a woman beside her, Leerah couldn't help but tune in to the conversation behind her.

"Isn't that your baby daddy's ex?" she heard someone ask.

"Mhm. That looks like her," another woman answered.

Leerah's contoured brows dipped. She had one baby daddy, and up until now, she was certain he only had two baby mamas. Convinced that they had to be discussing someone else, Leerah continued facing the direction she was in.

"Yeah, that's her. I don't know what T saw in her."

There was only one person she knew of that called Terrance by his first initial. Realizing who it was talking about her, Leerah turned around. She never cared enough about Ashley to scroll her page, but she knew what she looked like. Noticing her pretty dark skin and stacked body, it was clear that Terrance had a type.

Ashley saw exactly what Terrance saw in her. Leerah was gorgeous in person. If they were cool, she would've complimented her and asked what perfume she was wearing. It smelled divine.

"I couldn't help but overhear you talking about

my son's father," Leerah said, not beating around the bush.

"You sure he isn't T's godbrother's?" Ashley said.

Leerah couldn't help but scoff at how ridiculous she sounded. "Girl, please play with somebody else. I been wanting to beat a bitch up all week and you gon' get lucky."

"Hold on," Toni said, setting her drink down. "What's the problem?"

Ashley didn't acknowledge her but kept her focus on Leerah. "You know what, that was childish of me. We were talking about him."

"And he's your baby daddy?" Leerah challenged.

"Would've been. I, um... he made me get an abortion."

Either she was lying or didn't want to expose her hand. It didn't matter to Leerah, but she knew Terrance well enough to know he was just like his father— having a bunch of kids was his goal. *Maybe he didn't want any with her,* Leerah thought. Not knowing what to do with that information, Leerah picked up her drink.

"Oh, that's unfortunate. *For the both of us,* she thought. "But to answer you and your homegirl's question, yes, it's me in the flesh—no need to keep wondering," she said with a smile. "Have a good one."

Leerah walked off, slightly bothered by the news she just received. Truthfully, Leerah thought the girl should've been happy that she hadn't had a child by Terrance. The single parent life with him gone was no walk in the park and she wouldn't wish it on anyone. As she approached their section, she couldn't help but wonder if that's why Terrance was with Ashley the night he passed. *Had he made her get an abortion to save his family but wanted to take care of her,* Leerah thought. He was known to coddle a woman's feelings, including Leerah's, so she didn't put it past him.

"The bar must've been packed," Nae said.

Leerah drank her drink like it was a glass of water. She was trying not to let her nerves get the best of her. Yet again, Terrance had her out here looking silly, and she couldn't curse his ass out.

"It was," Toni replied. "I had to almost break up an ass-whooping, too."

"Oh, goodness. Who said something to you?" Sovanna asked Leerah.

She giggled. "Now, why did it have to be me? I was minding my business."

"And someone else was minding it, too," Toni added.

"That part. We ran into Ashley."

Nae blinked slowly. "Who is that?"

"The girl Terrance was with that night."

She mouthed "Oh" silently and nodded. Now she remembered her name. "What did she want?"

"Some fucking attention, so I gave it to her. She and her friend were insinuating that Terrance was her baby daddy, so I asked her."

"Oh, hell no. He got her pregnant?" Sovanna hissed.

"I guess so, but who knows? She said he made her get an abortion."

Nae grunted and crossed her legs. "A man can't make me do a damn thing."

"Oh, we know, honey." Toni laughed.

"Are you okay?" Sovanna asked.

She knew running into her had to be a bit traumatic.

Leerah nodded. "Yes, girl. It is what it is. I'm not worried about little fetus deletus."

Nae accidentally spit out some of her drink. She hurriedly grabbed some napkins and patted her legs. Toni and Sovanna had tears in their eyes from laughing so hard.

"You're going to hell. Let me scoot away from you," Toni wheezed, wiping her mouth.

Leerah shrugged. "So is she."

It was all jokes, but Leerah couldn't front like running into Ashley didn't help answer some questions she had. Ashley hadn't come out and said it, but Leerah knew. Terrance had made her get an abortion so he could make things right with her. All that begging and pleading, making promises to do right by her, was because he had royally screwed up. He knew if she found out he was having a baby with someone else, any thought of a relationship with him would've been a wrap, like the end of a movie scene.

As the night continued and Leerah consumed one more drink, she had one person on her mind. Since they'd agreed to take things slowly and as friends, Cree abided by her requests. His calls and texts were now responded to, and Leerah wanted to kick herself for ignoring him. Thankfully, her feelings were now sorted out, and she missed him. Grabbing her phone off the table, she glanced at the time, not realizing how late it'd gotten.

"Wow. It's almost one in the morning," she mumbled, going to her text messages. "Oh, well. I'm still about to text him."

Not knowing exactly what she wanted to say but knew what she was feeling, she sent him the eyes emoji. Between the liquor in her system and the slow jams playing, Leerah was ready to lay up. Before she could sit her phone back down, Cree replied. She beamed at his message.

Yes, Princess? I'm up.

Immediately, he was ready to tend to her needs.

I want to see you.

I've been drinking a lil' bit.

Can you come get me?

Her fingers moved swiftly over the screen as she triple-texted him. There was no shame in how she was feeling. On the other end of the phone, Cree chuckled. He could feel her urgency to see him through the screen, and he loved that shit.

Where you at?

No longer wanting to text him, Leerah stood up from the couch. She needed to hear his voice and see his face.

"Where are you going?" Sovanna asked, stifling a yawn.

"To make a call. Y'all not ready to go?"

Nae nodded. "I am. I know Toni is, too. Look at her."

She sat across from them, rubbing her right knee. Toni was the oldest, and these late nights were no longer her thing. She couldn't wait to shower and climb into her bed.

"I can hear y'all," she said, making them chuckle.

"We're ready to go whenever you are," Nae said.

Toni stood up. She was ready to leave thirty minutes ago but didn't want to ruin their fun. She went to use the bathroom, which she was glad was clean, and then they headed out. The cool night air refreshed them after being surrounded by clouds of smoke all night. The smell of tacos permeated the air as well.

"I did not know this taco truck stayed open this late," Sovanna said, pointing out the orange and green truck.

"Y'all want something?" Nae asked. "'Cause I do."

They served food in the lounge, but they didn't

order any and were glad they hadn't. There was nothing like eating authentic tacos with your eyes closed after a night out.

"I'm good," Leerah said. "I'll just wait for y'all right here."

"You sure? Because I don't need you reaching for nothing on my plate once I get mine," Nae said seriously.

Laughing, Leerah waved her off. "Trust me; I won't."

"All right. We'll be right back," Nae said.

Toni hit the locks on her car. "You can sit with me in the car and wait on them."

"I'm good, girl. I'ma enjoy this nice breeze," Leerah replied.

Nodding, Toni hopped in the driver's seat and started her car. Leerah swiped through her call log, locating Cree's name. The thought of him being with another woman at this hour hadn't crossed Leerah's mind until then, but it was too late. If he was laid up, he shouldn't have texted her back. The FaceTime call rang for two seconds before it connected. Cree's handsome face appeared on the screen, making Leerah smile giddily.

"Creeee," she sang, making him smirk.

"What's up, Princess. You feeling good?"

Leerah nodded and licked her lips. Cree lay bare chest in his bed with a black du-rag tied around his head and a gold cross chain around his neck. She couldn't remember the last time she'd seen him like this, but she wasn't complaining. He wiped the evident sleep out of his eyes and cleared his throat.

"I'm a lil' tipsy. I thought you were coming to get me?" Leerah questioned.

Cree's mouth opened wide as he yawned, and then he licked his lips. Leerah shivered. She had never found an action so sexy. Leave it to Cree to change her mind.

"I am," he said, tossing the white sheet off his body and climbing out of the bed. "You never told me what hookah lounge you were at."

"You know that new one in Overland Park? It just opened a few months ago."

He slid on a pair of sweat shorts, untied his du-rag, and chuckled. "The name, baby?"

Leerah almost gasped but held it in. The name slipped so casually from his mouth that it stunned her. Cree didn't even notice he'd said it.

"Oh yes. It's um," she said, facing the building and its glowing sign. "It's called Elite."

He nodded, recalling hearing the name in

conversation with a few of his boys. "A'ight. I'll be there in a minute. You good?"

She smirked. "Mhm. Are you good? Did I wake you up? Probably not. It's the weekend, so I'm sure you had some floozies on your line to keep you awake."

Cree chuckled lowly. "Nah. I was just waiting for your call."

"Right," Leerah said, giggling. "Tell me anything."

"I was. You see, I hit you right back when you texted me."

Women were on his line, in his inbox, and even in his business email, but none captured his attention. None of them, including the ones from his past, could hit him up and get him out of bed to pick them up. So, she had nothing to be worried about.

Leerah went to respond but got distracted by an engine revving from the opposite side of the parking lot. Squinting, she tried to see if she recognized anyone.

"What you staring at?" Cree asked, grabbing his gun and keys off the counter before entering his garage.

"Did Saleem get a new car?" Leerah asked.

"Yeah. Why?"

Shaking her head, she watched as someone who looked like him hopped out of a clean-ass charcoal gray Maserati MC20. The way he strolled over to whom Leerah assumed was Amira with a sexy, confident bop in his step made her wish she was closer. Nae and Sovanna rushed over with bottles of water in their hands, confirming what she was witnessing.

"Ooh. I know he didn't just snatch her up like that," Nae commented.

"He sure the fuck did. Should we go over there?" Leerah asked.

The sound of Cree telling her no drew her attention back to her phone. She'd forgotten all about him while trying to be nosey.

"Nah. Mind y'all business," he asserted. "They're grown and married."

"Oop." Sovanna chuckled. "I heard that. Hey, Cree."

Leerah held the phone toward them, and he bobbed his head upward. "What's up with it."

"You're just too coo' for us, honey," Nae cackled. "Where you headed?"

Leerah moved the phone out of their face. "Un, un. You asking too many questions."

Nae and Sovanna fell into one another laughing.

"Girl! I asked one question. Don't nobody care about him coming to get you," Nae hollered.

"Please come and get her!" Sovanna added, laughing. "She needs some dick!"

Cree expected Leerah to deny her claims, but she did the opposite.

"Yep. Sure do, and he the nigga that's gon' give me some," Leerah said boldly.

Sovanna and Nae both screamed. "I know that's right!"

"Baby, y'all are clowning." Toni chuckled after rolling her window down. "Go check on y'all food before I leave y'all."

"You ain't leaving nobody. Come on, Vanna," Nae said.

The duo walked off, getting stopped by a few men hanging around in the parking lot. Leerah looked back at the screen, and Cree glanced her way before focusing on the road.

"What you been sipping on?" he asked.

What he really wanted to ask her was how she figured she was getting some dick... as his friend. That was the real question.

"Gin and tequila," she answered.

Cree blew out an audible breath. "That's a

dangerous mixture. You trying to have a hangover, huh?"

"No." She chuckled. "I took a BC powder so I should be fine. Plus, those drinks are wearing off anyway."

"Yeah... we gon' see. Your hair looks nice," he complimented.

She simpered at his words. "Thank you."

"You're welcome. I'll be there in like six minutes."

"Okay. You can stay on this phone and talk to me," Leerah sassed.

Cree chuckled. "I wasn't hanging up. Just telling you my ETA."

"Mmmhmm. You not gon' believe who I ran into in there."

"Somebody you shouldn't have," Cree said.

Leerah bucked her eyes. "Yep. That girl, Ashley, Terrance was fucking with found herself next to me at the bar. I wasn't going to say anything at first, but she mentioned Terrance's name, trying to be funny, so I made her feel like a real clown. Did you know he got her pregnant?"

She was rambling, talking a mile per minute, but Cree listened. It was clear she needed him to hear her.

"Nah. I didn't know that," Cree replied truthfully.

He spotted her out and had his assumptions, but he wasn't privy to anything else. Terrance had only told him enough about her and brought her around enough to make it seem like she was nothing serious. To Terrance, she wasn't, but he slipped up and got her pregnant.

"Yeah, well, she was, and he made her get an abortion, thinking it was going to keep me. Tuh. She could've kept that lil' baby if anything."

Cree didn't have anything to say, so he didn't—not on the topic, at least. "Is this you by the white Lexus?" he asked.

Leerah's eyes scanned the lot and spotted him pulling in. "Yes."

Cree pulled his black, heavily tinted Lucid Air a few spaces over and parked. Licking his lips, he watched her strut over to him, looking too fine for words. He rolled his window down as she approached the car with a smile.

"Did someone request a driver?" Cree jested.

Leerah chuckled. "You got here fast. Hey," she said softly, feeling her stomach flutter with him now in her presence.

"Hello, to you, too," he greeted huskily. His eyes swept appreciatively over her frame. "You ready?"

"Yeah. Let me say bye to the girls."

Cree nodded and kept his eyes on her as she returned to Toni's car. Sovanna and Nae waved as they approached with their food in plastic bags.

"What kind of car is that?" Nae asked. "It's clean as hell."

"An electric car. It's called a Lucid I think," Leerah answered. "It rides real smooth."

Sovanna smirked. "Mhm. I'm sure that's not the only thing that rides smooth."

"Shut up! I don't know about all that, but I'ma find out," Leerah said.

"I thought you just wanted to remain friends?" Nae asked.

Leerah smiled. "I'm testing the waters. We agreed on that."

"Oh," Nae chirped. "Well, that's good. Don't drown."

"You need to be telling him that," Leerah said, making them laugh before giving them hugs. "Text me when y'all get home."

"Which home?" Sovanna questioned, giggling. "I'm going straight to my man's house. And I got the code to the alarm."

"Look at you, moving on up. He gon' give your ass a baby next!" Leerah hollered, backpedaling.

"And I'ma keep it, too!" Sovanna shouted after her. "Love you!"

"Love you too!"

She climbed into his car, still smiling. Cree glanced her way. "We going to your crib or mine?"

"Mine," Leerah answered breathily.

"A'ight. Buckle up," he instructed, shifting gears. "You need to stop for anything first?"

Leerah shook her head and fastened her seatbelt. "No. Do you?"

"Nah. I got everything I need right next to me."

Leerah grinned all the way to her house, not realizing how true his words were.

EVERMORE
SERIES

A wave of déjà vu hit Cree as he sat on Leerah's sectional. Despite it being two in the morning, she was still wide awake and being a great host. A half bottle of Don Julio and two shot glasses sat on her living room table while *What's On Your Mind* by K CAMP played on the TV. Leerah laid out beside him with her feet on his lap, receiving a massage.

Cree hit a spot in her foot that made a moan slip from her lips.

His slow, pressured caress paused, gauging any further reaction. The rise and fall of her chest, led his hands to venture up her calf. Leerah's head lolled to one side in pure bliss.

"That feel good?" he questioned, watching her chest rise and fall slowly.

She didn't bother to open her eyes. "Mhm. I forgot how good at this you are."

Cree smirked. She seemed to have forgotten a lot of things between them, and tonight, he was ready to remind her. Leerah's eyes fluttered behind their lids as Cree skillfully used his hands. She complained that her feet hurt when they stepped inside the house, and three minutes later, he was solving her problem.

Now, she had another one he needed to handle. The moisture between her thighs was embarrassing and only getting worse. His hands moved from her feet up to her calves, kneading them with expertise as if he'd attended college to be a therapist. He hadn't. Cree had multiple degrees in business and marketing, but Leerah was positive he returned to become a masseuse.

With each groove he hit, Cree caught a whiff of

the perfume she spritzed on her ankles earlier in the night. It meshed perfectly with the scent of her arousal. Feeling herself unconsciously spread spreading her legs, Leerah quickly sat up. Cree looked at her like he'd done something wrong.

"You good?" he asked.

"Yeah. I was about to fall asleep," she fibbed, standing up. "Ooh. This is my song."

Grabbing the remote, she turned up the volume to a song she had given far too many guys dances to during her first few years in college. *Dumptruck* by Kinfolk Thugs would forever take her back to those good ol' days when she heard it. Snapping her fingers, Leerah rolled her hips, putting a dip in her back as if she were backing it up on someone. She placed both hands on her knees and grinded slowly to the beat. Cree sat with his legs spread and a grin that couldn't be contained.

"You not gon' stand up and dance with me?" Leerah cheesed, tossing her hair over her shoulder.

Cree shook his head. "You know I ain't the dancing type."

"Of course, you're not," she said playfully, rolling her eyes. "You used to come to the parties and post up for no reason."

"Damn. I couldn't just want to enjoy the scenario?" He laughed.

"Sure, Cree. Enjoy it."

Leerah continued dancing, enticing him and testing his boundaries. They weren't in their twenty-somethings anymore. Cree went out back then because he had nothing else to do. As a college athlete, he didn't care to be on the scene every weekend, but his presence was welcomed when he did step out.

As for Leerah, she lived her best life all four years, but especially when she lived in the dorms. That seemed like so long ago, not but those memories.... They never faded. She cherished them, and so did Cree—especially the ones with her. Leerah had more ass and hips than a little bit now. When she reached for another shot, Cree tugged at the hem of her dress.

"Come show me somethin'," he coaxed, tugging her until she fell into his lap.

Giggling, Leerah adjusted herself on him. Hands now on his thighs, she rolled her hips. Cree's hand traveled down her hip and over the top of her round ass. Her dress lifted with each sultry swirl, but neither of them lowered it. The more she danced, the harder Cree's dick got underneath her. Freakily, Leerah pressed harder into him.

In her mind, dry humping wasn't a lost art to Leerah. It was an act so sensually vulnerable, with its heavy breathing and longing stares. There was a yearning for so much more, not knowing when they'd get it.

Arching her back, Leerah held onto the edge of the table and made her ass bounce. Looking back at him, she smirked. Cree had his eyes trained on her round cheeks, which were now fully exposed. Sensually, he rubbed them, spreading them wide as she made them clap. Her black thong played peek-a-boo, and Cree slid his finger underneath it, gaining a sneak peek at her slick pussy lips.

"That pussy still pretty," he mumbled, sliding his hand across her mound and patting it.

Leerah stumbled, but he caught her. She sat back down on his lap, leaning against his chest. Nastily, Cree licked up the side of her neck while palming her breasts, massaging them. When he tweaked her nipples, Leerah bit into her bottom lip, and her eyes rolled.

"Mmm," she moaned softly.

"You want me to stop?"

Leerah opened her eyes at the sound of his voice.

She felt intoxicated and not from the liquor she'd been sipping. Neither of them noticed that the song had ended. All they heard was each other's heavy breathing. Standing up, she tugged her dress down and walked around the table. She needed to put some distance between them for a second.

Cree adjusted his dick and licked his lips. "What's the matter?"

Her comfort always mattered to him.

"Let's um... slow it down for a second. Can we play a game?"

He cleared his throat. "You not tired of playing those?"

Appalled, Leerah's mouth opened and stayed like that for seconds before she laughed. "Don't do that."

"I'm just saying. You been playing a lot of games with me," he said, teasingly.

"Okay, but we said we would test the waters first."

"And that shit is wet *and* warm," Cree explained, making her laugh. "You laughing, and I'm ready to go swimming. Bring your ass here."

"No, wait!" she screeched when he looked like he was about to stand up. "Let me tell you the game first, and I promise I'm done."

He got comfortable on the couch. "You take your princess role so seriously," he jested.

"You should've never given me the name." She shrugged. "Now, the game is called two truths and a lie. We'll tell each other three statements about ourselves, and we have to guess which ones are a lie or the truth. If you get it right, I have to take a shot and vice versa."

"Nah. I ain't fucking with you and that liquor," he said, making Leerah laugh.

She always knew when Cree was intoxicated because he cursed more.

"Okay, then what?"

"How many rounds are we playing?" he asked.

She hadn't thought that far yet. "Hmm. Let's do ten. That's five turns a piece."

"A'ight. We can take shots the first two rounds and then strip after that."

"Strip?" Leerah repeated. "Clothes?" She needed clarification.

"What else, baby? I almost had your pretty ass up out of that dress anyway. Let's play." Cree clapped his hands and grinned, knowing he was about to win.

Leerah groaned, contemplating backing out and just giving him what she knew they both wanted, but she didn't. They were both competitive, so she was ready to see how good he thought he knew about her.

"I'm going first," she quipped.

Cree smirked. "Of course, ladies first. You know I'm a gentleman."

"Yeah, yeah. Okay... let's see," she pondered. She didn't want to make it easy for him at all. "I graduated summa cum laude, my first car was a Volkswagen Beetle, and I cut one of my ponytails off when I was five."

Thinking hard, Cree squinted, resting a hand on his chin. "Damn...okay. I do remember you being real smart in college, so summa cum laude isn't a far stretch."

Leerah laughed, and his eyes expanded.

"What you laughing for? That shit wrong, isn't it?"

She giggled. "I can't tell you. Finish."

He shook his head. "I can see you cutting your hair like a badass kid, so that's the truth. You pushing a Beetle? Nah. I couldn't see that. So that's a lie."

Beaming, Leerah grabbed the bottle and poured him a shot. "You lost."

"Ain't no way. What was a lie?"

"Cutting my hair. I knew better." She chuckled. "My first car was a Beetle, thank you very much. I named her Benita."

Cree grabbed the shot from her extended hand and tossed it back. "I should've known that. It's all good, though. My turn."

"I'm ready. You gon' be naked and drunk when we're finished."

He chuckled. "Yeah, we'll see. A'ight... my middle name is Hezekiah, I'm allergic to blueberries, and I'm ambidextrous."

"Oh, my gosh. Wait! How can I not remember your middle name?" She pondered, sitting up on her knees. "You've told me before, right?"

"Possibly. You ain't got all day." He chuckled.

"Fine! I truly believe that you're ambidextrous. My feet are still tingling. Hezekiah," she said, mumbling the word to see if it sounded like something his mama would name him. "That's a lie, and you are allergic to blueberries."

Cree smiled. "You're correct."

Leerah clapped. "Of course, I am. Can you tell me your middle name again?"

"It's Hiram."

"Cree Hiram Landry. I like, I like."

Chuckling, he said, "You know we share the same first and last initials just flipped."

She thought about it for a few seconds. "Leerah

Canady and Cree Landry. The spellings are almost the same, too. That's..."

"Kismet," he said and winked. "Your turn."

"Un, un. You have to strip since I won. We're on round three."

Cree nodded. "You're right."

He only slipped on a tank top when he left to pick her up, and he removed that first. Leerah swallowed hard, eyeing his taut stomach. Seeing it over the phone was nothing compared to in person. Not letting him distract her, she shook away the lustful fuzziness that clouded her brain. She asked if he was ready, and Cree nodded.

"Okay. I've never had a crush on anyone, I learned to drive when I was thirteen, and I used to be obsessed with Tweety Bird."

Cree wasted no time with his answers.

"Two truths... Tweety Bird and you learning to drive at thirteen. The lie...you've been crushing on me since you stepped into our African American studies class," he answered smoothly.

Without hesitation, he pulled Leerah's card. Cree remembered the first day they encountered one another. She was running late, and the last seat was by him. Cree had been saving it for one of his homeboys from the track team, but Leerah had ever so kindly asked him if she could sit there. It became her permanent spot for the remainder of the semester.

"Just call me out, why don't you." She chuckled, standing to her feet. "Can I take a shot or…"

"Or nothing. Take that dress off, and let me see somethin', Princess."

Cree poured him another shot while Leerah slowly unbuttoned her dress. Her movements lagged as if she weren't ready to part ways with the only garment that kept her concealed. She was exposing herself more than she already had—not just physically, either. Cree had tapped into a side of her that Leerah no longer wanted to keep hidden.

She had a softer, vulnerable side that she was okay with letting him witness. Having her guard up all the time was exhausting, and life had tired her enough. Leerah felt deeply caressed from the inside out by Cree's eyes alone. She unfastened the last button and peeled the dress from her body. It fell to the ground, revealing a pink and black bra and a black thong.

Her body was thicker and softer in places, carrying an allure that attracted Cree to her more than ever. Standing before him, she carried herself with the utmost confidence. Motherhood made her curves more pronounced, and Cree's heart swelled with admiration for the mother that she was. She'd adapted to the demands, risking it all to bring a life into this world and still maintained an innate sensuality that had him ready to give her the world.

Her body didn't just tell a story of birth. Its dips and curves narrated growth, love, strength, and, most of all, resilience. Cree felt privileged to bear witness to such beauty, and he let her know it.

"Beautiful body to match your beautiful soul, Princess. You got it," he praised.

Leerah grazed her neck with the back of her hand. "Thank you. It's your turn."

She didn't know it, but this was the last round of statements Cree was giving her.

"I'm a lover boy at heart, I take care of the people I love, and I've never gotten the taste of you off my mind."

Leerah was breathing until his last statement. Her lips slightly parted but no words came out. She didn't have any to say that could dispute his truths. Every last one was a fact and he didn't need to explain them for her to know it.

"Cree," she breathed, afraid to say anything else.

"Tell me the lie, Princess."

She swallowed hard and blinked fast. "None... none of them are a lie."

"So, I lost for playing unfair?"

Leerah nodded, and he stood from the couch.

"That means I have to strip."

In one steady motion, Cree lowered his shorts and black Polo briefs. Leerah placed a hand against her chest, but it really should've covered her mouth. Or her eyes. She didn't feel grown enough to be seeing Cree in this light. Or the light his dick had hidden with the shadow it created. Every bold bone in her body weakened at the sight of it bobbing freely, telling her to come here.

Cree was 95% dick and 5% body.

Leerah was convinced that all the working out at the gym and the food he ate traveled right where it belonged, between his legs. He was packing heavily like a woman did her suitcase for a three-day vacation. It was extra everything— sickening veins, impressive length, proud girth, daunting weight, and *extra* fucking pretty in its chocolate hue. The sad thing was, Leerah knew he wasn't fully hard and that excited her more.

"I mean... you didn't have to strip," Leerah said as they, him and his third leg, walked up to her.

"We done playing games?"

She nodded. "Yes."

Liking her answer, Cree kissed her lips, slipping

his tongue inside her mouth. He could tell she'd been wanting him to do so all night, so he put her out of her misery. His movements were languorous and intentional, swiping every corner of her mouth to savor her taste. Kissing him that night wasn't a mistake, and he needed Leerah to know that.

Through the speakers, Pretty Willie's sonorous voice on *4Walls* became the soundtrack to their make-out session. Cree wanted to make good on his lyrics and focus on only them for the night... and the present. He was done living in the past. With a firm grip on her plush ass and his dick pressing into her stomach, Cree broke their lip-lock.

"Let's go to the bedroom."

Leerah had never been happier to hear those words.

"AIN'T NO GOING BACK AFTER THIS."

NINE

The moment Leerah lay on the bed after Cree removed her bra and thong, she realized that she'd been having sex incorrectly. Technically, there was no one way or wrong way to engage in the activity, but there was a right way. She became a student of the game as Cree gave her a lesson on lovemaking.

He took his time tending to her body like he did when he spoke, speaking to it in a language only he understood. Soon, she'd learn it, too. Fluently, expertly, his lips left their mark down her neck. The warmth of his tongue against her skin set her ablaze, exhaling needy and desperate breaths. She didn't want him to stop.

When he made it to her breasts, Cree wasn't prepared for the sweetness of them. A foreign yet welcomed taste greeted him as he sucked gingerly. Cupping one and then the other in his hands, he bounced them in his face. Leerah giggled.

"I love these big pretty mothafuckas," he whispered, kissing and licking them.

Focusing on one, he twirled his tongue around her areola before trying to stuff his face full. This was exactly where he wanted to end his night; on her chest while she rubbed his waves. Cree went back to sucking hard on her nipples, trying not to let the heat from between her legs distract him. It almost did until a trickle of liquid hit his tastebuds. He knew what it was without asking and kept on pleasing her.

When she winced and let out a whiny moan, Cree lifted his head. "Am I hurting you?"

She quickly shook her head. "No. They're sensitive, but it feels so good."

He nodded and ducked his head to continue. Leerah didn't care for nipple stimulation as much, but Cree was making her love it. She only teased them when she was PMS'ing because that's when they hurt the most. Something about the slight pain brought her an immense amount of pleasure. Cree had tapped into that, too, biting and sucking at her tenderness.

Removing his mouth, he brushed a thumb over both nipples and kissed down her stomach. Lingering, he caressed her belly, peppering it with kisses that made Leerah blush behind her hand. One hand stayed there as he mumbled words Leerah couldn't make out. He said a quick prayer over her womb, knowing and believing that one day a life created by the love shared between them would reside there.

Cree shook his head as he kissed her heated thighs. The smell of her had him high like he'd popped a pill. He spread them to his liking, and Leerah's breath hitched when his tongue glided over her slickness.

She hadn't been touched by anyone else but herself in months. Nine, to be exact. Cree slid one, two, then three fingers inside her. He didn't immediately take her clit into his mouth. Savoring her scent and warmth, Cree languidly swayed his head from side to side, covering himself in her juices. With each turn of direction, he delivered drawn-out licks. His tongue was so thick, Leerah felt like it covered her entire pussy with each swipe.

"Uuuh," she groaned, hips lifting from the mattress.

Using one arm, Cree pulled her body back down and deeper into his mouth by her thighs. She'd been running from him long enough; tonight wasn't the night to do so. Rapid flicks of his tongue made her buck against him, but she didn't run.

"Yeah," Cree mumbled. "Feed me this pussy."

Leerah shoved it in his face, humping it like she'd never be given the chance to again. Cree slapped her thigh, forcing her to relax. He'd given her instructions but was still running the show. Softly, with the utmost love, he ate her pussy and kept a firm grip on her hips so she couldn't run. His silent dominance made her melt in his mouth.

"Oh, my gosh," she moaned, pressing her head into the mattress.

Her breathy sounds only made him go harder, suck longer, and dig deeper. Detaching his drenched fingers from inside her, Cree placed them at her lips. Leerah opened her mouth, sucking her juices from his fingers. Removing them, he placed his fingertips on her clit and rubbed like he was trying to remove a stain from the counter. Leerah's body twitched, and her legs trembled.

"Yeeessss!" she screamed out as an orgasm rocked her entire being.

Replacing his fingers with his mouth, Cree sucked her clit into his mouth. He loved the feel of it throbbing against his tongue. This was orgasm number two, and he had a few more he wanted to pull up out of her. Lifting his head, he sat back on his hunches, observing, admiring her flustered body. Leerah squeezed her breasts while squeezing her legs shut. The aftershock of her climax had her delirious.

Cree hovered over her, placing his hands over hers. "You gon' let me slide my dick in between these, Princess?"

"Yes."

He kissed her lips, letting her taste more of herself. In no rush to leave her mouth, they kissed slowly. Leerah's body reacted to him in a way she'd only imagined in her mind. Cree had complete control as their tongues tangled, and her legs circled his trim waist. Without speaking, he showed that he desired her. It was in the thrusting of his tongue in her mouth, the ravenous bites to her bottom lip, and the movement of his hips between her legs. She'd finally decoded the language he had spoken to her in earlier.

Waves of pleasure rolled over her as he glided his dick along her slickness. He knew sliding in her without a rubber was absolute insanity, but he wanted to lose his mind. Lose complete control.

Leerah could become the sole owner of it without thought.

"You on birth control?"

She nodded, and his dick grew harder.

"Fuck, baby," Cree groaned.

He slid just the tip across her clit, battling with himself. The plan wasn't to make her a mother of two, but he'd do it. Not because he was selfish like that, but because Leerah wasn't playing fair. She stroked him herself, dipping his dick in and out of her warmth like they'd discussed.

"Test the temperature. It's *so* warm inside," Leerah cooed, licking his neck. She sucked on it, biting the skin, before kissing his Adam's apple.

"I'm clean," he assured her.

"I am, too. I haven't had sex since last year."

Cree could tell. He struggled to slide his fingers inside her. Scooting them to the edge of the bed, Cree climbed off it. Pressing her legs back, he dropped his heavy dick against her mound. Leerah felt the tip of him almost reach the top of her stomach and it quivered. *This man is about to break me in half. I know it,* she thought happily.

"Ain't no going back after this," he declared, slapping his length against her clit.

To let him know that she knew that Leerah

reached down and stroked him. "I know. Give me this dick."

Cree struggled to ease inside of her. No amount of lubrication could have prepared him for how fucking tight she was. His nostrils flared as he inhaled a sharp breath. The grunts and groans he released while sliding deeply in and out of her drove Leerah insane.

He took a moment to relish in their connection. The view of her creaminess coating his Black dick was art. The type of masterpiece you had to admire silently because it was just that damn breathtaking. Cree didn't talk much while he was in it, but he damn sure didn't have to. That dick was doing all the talking.

Leerah gasped. "Uuh fuck! Yes!"

He dipped in and out of her, long stroking like the swimmer he was. Pressing her knees into the bed with her pretty toes on his chest, Cree cusped underneath her breasts and pounded into her. She wanted to watch him slide in and out of her but failed. Leerah's head fell back, and hands gripped her hair. She covered her face trying to hide from him, but Cree wasn't having that.

"Move them hands and hold your feet," he commanded.

Leerah's head thrashed against the bed. "I...I can't."

"Yes, you can. Hold 'em. I ain't gon' tell you again."

Her hands gripped her feet without further instruction. Seeing her wet his dick up as he slid in and out of her made Cree have crazy thoughts. Anybody who brought her pain and any type of suffering was going to have to see him. He was willing to fall out with whoever about Leerah and her good-ass pussy. Morals and relationship history be damned.

"Cree! Oh, my gosh! Creeeee! You gon make me cuuum," Leerah whined like it was a problem.

Cree stared down at her pretty, contorted face. Those words were the sweetest harmony. He kept his pace and didn't switch up until Leerah dropped her feet and squirted all over him, the bed, and the floor.

"That's what the fuck I'm talking about, Princess. Wet this dick up," Cree encouraged.

He swiped his dick over her pussy, making her leak even more. Cree had the type of dick that placed you in a straitjacket. When he flipped her over without so much as a word and slid back inside her, Leerah knew she was down bad. Cree gripped her sweated silk press, forcing the arch in her back to deepen.

Smack!

"Let me stretch this pussy out," Cree insisted.

"Oooh. Stretch it out," Leerah moaned, looking over her shoulder at him.

Cree smacked her ass again, making their skin clap loudly. She looked so good throwing her ass back, he wished he had his phone to record them. Coming up on her hands, she remained eye contact and met him thrust for thrust. Slowing it down, she twirled her hips.

"Mmhmm. Yeah...Look how good you look fucking me. You gon' make me act a fool in this shit." Cree huffed.

He pressed her back down, forcing Leerah's chest to lay flat on the bed. Leerah's screams of pleasure made him fuck her harder. Cree thumbed her asshole, and she came again. He stroked her senseless for a minute straight, enjoying how her ass wobbled and tightness engulfed him.

The backshots he was delivering had her seeing stars, and Leerah wondered how much it'd cost to name one after him. He rightfully earned that spot in the sky. The way her walls hugged his dick, Cree promised to never keep it away from her. When he pulled all the way out and stroked himself, Leerah whined.

"Nooo. Put it back in," she begged.

Cree slid back inside her and spanked her ass. "Be quiet. I ain't going nowhere."

He pounded into her, tossing nothing but dick in her guts. Cree needed her to feel every inch. And she was taking it, too. Leerah fisted the sheets, holding on for dear life. When he slowed his pace and let her take control, Cree felt his toes tingle.

"Sss," he hissed, biting into his bottom lip. "You feel so good. Fuck," he groaned, drawing out the word with a rasp.

Leerah rocked her hips, sliding to the tip and back down. The erotic sounds of her wetness heightened her arousal. She was making a fucking mess on his dick, and Cree loved it.

"Yeah... just like that. Look at me while you cum on this dick."

Her head turned as she moaned with stuttered breaths. Cree flexed his jaw, and her eyes fluttered. Reaching under her, Leerah rubbed her clit as his hands moved lovingly down the length of her back.

"This my dick?" she asked.

His eyes met hers. The way she was putting the pussy on him, Cree could only groan and nod. She fucked him harder and faster.

"Tell me. Mmm, tell me it's mine," she moaned.

Cree smacked her ass. "This your dick forever. Now make it nut."

"Give me a kiss."

He leaned over her, still delivering AI pipe, and tongued her down. There was something so erotic and romantic about kissing while he was in it that Leerah loved. She contracted around him and felt Cree pulse. He moaned inside her mouth, gripping her waist as he came. His heavy breathing made Leerah grin as he stayed resting against her back. She curled into his body as he massaged her slick skin. When he did pull his mouth off hers, Cree nestled in the crook of her neck and held her tight.

"What you smiling for?" he asked, feeling her grin against his cheek.

"I told you you'd be the one giving me some dick."

Chuckled, Cree kissed her neck. "You a fool, Princess."

"I'm glad you know."

EVERMORE
SERIES

Leerah wasn't sure what time they'd fallen asleep, but she was getting some of the best rest in her life. Cree held her naked frame against his. His lower half was covered in his shorts, having retrieved them hours earlier when Leerah went to use the bathroom. They were knocked out without a care in the world. Vivid images of their past floated through Leerah's mind as she dreamed. It hadn't happened in years, but timing was everything.

The Past

Watching her dance freely around her living room, Cree shook his head. He knew this was a setup—maybe not on her end at first, but now he thought otherwise. Leerah was a tease and was making it difficult for Cree to keep the line of friendship between them.

"We're supposed to be studying," Cree said.

Leerah swung her head his way, curly hair giving him a whiff of its coconut and honey scent. Her leave-in conditioner had become his favorite to smell on her.

"We will. I like to play music to hype me up first," she said.

"And take showers," Cree mumbled, with eyes roaming her damp skin.

She told him to meet her at her dorm at a specific time, and he was there. Punctuality had been a trait of his for years— one Gramps had instilled in him. He realized it wasn't one of Leerah's from the day he met her. She was ten minutes late, which turned into thirty after she whined about needing a shower.

Cree was patient. He had no choice, considering they had to work on an assignment together. Leerah stealing his homeboy's seat in class turned into them eating lunch in between classes after they ran into one another in the Chick-fil-A line. They went from sharing meals to morning workouts, pre-gaming at Cree's crib, her attending his track meets, and some-times them falling asleep at one another's place.

They quickly became close friends, and Cree wondered if that's what they'd always be. Leerah was always her goofy, shit-talking self around him, so he didn't mind the friendship title. He had plenty of platonic friendships, but this one felt different. He could see it being something more if they decided to take it there.

"I just came from the gym! I told you that," Leerah fussed.

"With who?" he asked more harshly than he intended, not being able to stop himself.

Leerah stopped removing her books from her tote and stared at him. "Why?"

"What you mean why? I'm just asking a question."

Cree wasn't going to tell her a few of his team-mates had joked with him about seeing *his girl* working out with another guy. It wasn't against any unwritten friendship agreement they had stating she couldn't work out with someone else, but it was the principle. Cree had been waiting for her to bring it up in conversation since last week.

"But why did you say it like that?" Leerah asked, tugging on her spandex shorts.

Cree's eyes followed the movement. Her thighs were toned and distractingly thick with an ass that had the perfect shelf. He saw exactly why whoever the nigga was wanted to work out with her. Nose flaring, Cree shook his head.

"Never mind," he said, unzipping his backpack to grab his folder out. "It don't even matter."

"Awww," Leerah cooed, walking over to him. She stepped between his strong legs and stood directly in his face. "Is that baby jealous?"

"Never that. Work out with who you want to."

She tried taking his folder out of his hand, but he held onto it with a firm grip. Stubbornly, she kept tugging, so Cree let it go.

"But you don't want me to? Is that what it is?"

"Do what makes you feel comfortable, Leerah."

She gasped. "Why are you talking to me like that? I didn't even do anything."

The whine in her voice and pout on her face made Cree feel bad. He wasn't trying to hurt her feelings just because he was in his.

"You right. My bad," he said.

She placed the folder beside him on the couch. "Cree."

He sighed. "What, man? We're supposed to be studying and you standing here trying to do an analysis on why you think I'm jealous. I ain't. So, let it go."

Leerah felt like she had to puke, and her eyes

watered. Cree had never talked to her in this manner, and she didn't realize how much his words could affect her. His head snapped back as she mushed him hard in the forehead.

"Don't talk to me like that." Her voice quivered as she stormed off.

Cree hopped up from the couch. His long legs made it easy to catch her around the waist, turning her to face him. Tears pooled in her eyes, and Cree's heart sank to the soles of his Nike flip-flops.

"Aye," he said softly. "What you crying for?"

Leerah blinked, and a tear fell. Cree wiped it away as her chest hiccupped, and she shrugged.

"Yes, you do. Tell me," he urged.

"You just… made me feel bad talking to me like that. I didn't know it was a crime to work out with someone. Someone who is my friend."

Cree's jaw twitched. "You got a lot of friends, huh?"

"Cree," Leerah whined, rolling her eyes. "It's not like that. You're tripping."

"A'ight. I'll drop it."

"Please, do, because you have *friends* just like me."

"Just like you? What you mean by that?"

Leerah cocked her head to the side. "Let's not play crazy. Aren't you in a relationship?"

"Nah," he quickly denied. "Where you hear that from?"

"Doesn't matter. This entire conversation doesn't even matter because it shouldn't."

Cree gritted his teeth. "Yeah, 'cause friends shouldn't care about what other friends have going on in their lives even though it's not like that," he said. His words heavy with sarcasm.

She sucked her teeth. "Whatever. Admit you were tripping and say sorry for hurting my feelings so I can feel better."

Smirking, he licked his lips, ready to obey his pretty princess' orders. "I was tripping, and I'm sorry. You don't have to cry," he said, kissing her wet cheeks. "I'm sorry, okay?"

Leerah shook her head, no, and his silky brows dipped in confusion.

"No?" he quizzed.

"I don't feel better."

His eyes lowered in a dreamy gaze. The hand he still had settled at her waist toyed with the band of her shorts.

"What do I need to do to make you feel better?" Cree asked.

Leerah shrugged. Deep down, she knew exactly what she wanted him to do, and it involved his juicy ass lips.

"Whatever you want," she answered.

Cree's hand dipped inside her shorts and palmed her sex while keeping his eyes on her. Her lips parted as his fingers spread her lower set. She was *too* wet, and Cree wondered if she'd just been walking around like that upon his arrival. And why she didn't have any fucking panties on. *Yeah, this was a setup,* he thought.

Angling his body, he played in her wetness, swirling the stickiness over her clit and staying there. Applying pressure, Cree didn't have to tell her to widen her stance. Her legs accommodated him on their own.

"Uumm," Leerah moaned.

Her stomach caved when he slid a finger inside of her. He stroked her a few times, letting her enjoy the feel. When he slid another finger in, Leerah's chin dropped to her chest.

"Look at me," Cree said in a warm, commanding tone that made her eyes meet his.

His dick twitched as her eyes fluttered with the utmost appreciation for his skillful fingers. She was in awe by the way he pumped them in and out of her, creating a trail of juices rolling down his palm and wrist. Cree wanted to ask her if it felt good, but he knew it did. Pleasure was written all over her face.

Locating her G-spot, Cree caressed it, finessing his fingers in a way that had Leerah grip his shirt. Her breaths grew choppy as if she were choking on them. She drew a fist to her mouth and bit her knuckle, but Cree tugged her wrist.

"I want to hear you."

He pulsed his fingers against her spongy, sensitive area, and Leerah whimpered. "I'ma cum," she whispered, almost ashamed. Her grip on him tightened simultaneously with her walls. "Oh, my gosh. Cree! I'm cumming."

Her moans were muffled into his chest as she unraveled. She had his fingers in a death grip as she came all over them. Cree held onto her as her body twitched. She felt his dick pressing into her and went to slide her hand inside his shorts but stopped when his phone vibrated against the kitchen counter. He placed it on the charger when he came in.

Leerah lifted her head and glanced at it. Cree hadn't bothered to. He was focused on her. The name flashing on the screen was one of his *friends* Leerah had heard about. She wasn't sure if they were in a relationship, although he told her they weren't. Still, homegirl had ruined the moment.

Feeling her tense up, Cree slowly removed his hand from her shorts. He cleared his throat and watched as she adjusted them. She was flustered and annoyed, but she felt *so* much better. She watched in awe as Cree licked his fingers and then his lips.

"All better now?" he asked.

Leerah was speechless. She nodded, rubbing at a spot on the side of her neck. "Y-Yeah. Thanks, *friend.*"

C ree listened intently as Leerah moaned in her sleep. It was soft and lulling, but there was no going back to sleep. He was now wide awake despite the long night they had. Her body pressed more into his, fidgeting as if she were having a bad dream. It wasn't bad at all. It was wet, like her.

Her dream didn't get to the good part, but the reality was better—so much better. This time was different. They were grown, and there wasn't a young college girl blowing Cree's line down and interrupting them.

Peeling his eyes open, Cree wiped the sleep from them and observed her movements. Sunlight seeped through the blinds, giving him a perfect view of her beauty. His Sleeping Princess. Even in her inebriated state, she remembered to put her bonnet on last night. Her silk press wasn't the freshest anymore, but that was okay. Cree sweated it out and promised to get it redone.

Leerah's warm leg was draped over his, and the feeling of waking up to her was unmatched. A true blessing. Cree caressed her side, fingers dipping and massaging curves that slightly awakened her. He ran his palm along the swell of her heavy breast, brushing his thumb over her nipple. Leerah's head tilted. A hint of a smile present as she recognized his touch.

His hand traveled upward, causing goosebumps to coat her skin. Cree placed his hand on her neck but didn't squeeze; he just caressed it gently, lovingly. Warm lips kissed her cheek.

"Good morning," he rasped.

Leerah ran her foot up and down his hairy leg and smiled. "Good morning."

"Can I feed you this morning?" Cree asked.

She thought he was talking about food, and maybe he was, but not at the moment. Still, she nodded. He didn't know what to expect from her body last night or the way it responded to him, but

Cree was fully aware right now. He felt her warmth against his thigh. Underneath the cover, Cree tugged his shorts down. His morning wood saluted them both as it roughly poked her in the ass.

"Mmm. That's for me?" Leerah asked, reaching behind her to stroke him.

She patted it on her bare lips, and Cree pushed inside her. Feeling her cushiony walls in this position let him know he wasn't going to last long. Wiggling her cheek, he thrusted his hips, sliding in deep. Choking on a moan, Leerah placed a hand against his thigh.

"Baby," she whimpered.

Cree moved her hand out of the way. "You don't wanna take it?" He licked her neck, still feeding her dick.

"I do."

"Throw that fat ass back, then."

The smack to her left cheek encouraged her, and Leerah did as she was told. Her pussy was still swollen from hours earlier with the beating he put on it, so fucking him back didn't last long. Cree caught her sedated movements and pulled out of her. Tossing the comforter off them, Cree rolled Leerah onto her stomach. He kissed her shoulders and down her back.

"You just wanna lay here and take it? That's okay. I got you. Lift up," he instructed.

Cree slid a pillow underneath her, propping her ass higher in the air and at an angle for him to slide in deeper. He straddled her legs, rubbing her ass cheeks before positioning himself at her entrance.

"Mm, fuck," he moaned, watching his dick disappear.

Cree fucked her slowly, making Leerah's eyes roll. She lived up to her role, being a pillow princess for the moment, but still occasionally fucked him back from below. She didn't have to do much because Cree had it and her body under control. Leerah gripped her cheeks, opening herself up more for him. He quickly pulled out of her and slapped his dick against her backside.

"You almost made me nut, Princess," he expressed proudly.

"I wanna feel that nut, baby."

Cree slid back inside her, pressing her into the mattress. The slow lovemaking he was on earlier was gone. He delivered quick, steady strokes that had Leerah shouting. He smacked her ass hard.

"Oooh fuck! Yes, yes, yes. Don't stop."

"I'm not. I'ma cum all in this pussy."

And he meant that. Minutes later, with Leerah's

bonnet now missing, Cree ejaculated some inside her before pulling out and stroking the rest of his release onto her ass. She made her cheeks jiggle as he smeared the creaminess along her skin. Spreading her cheeks, he shook his head, watching their juices slip out of her and down her slit onto the bed.

"That was sexy," he complimented, smacking her ass.

Cree reclaimed his spot next to her and laid out. Leerah didn't want to move, but she knew she had to get up and wash him off of her. Turning her head, she smirked at the content expression on his face. They both shared that freshly fucked look. Leerah kissed the side of his mouth, and he turned his head to feel her lips.

"I needed that," she said. "How nice of you."

Cree chuckled. "You're welcome. What else you need?"

"A shower and some real food this time."

"I got you. It's this new spot we can slide to if you want," he suggested.

Leerah wasn't expecting him to suggest a public place, but she should've known better. He wasn't keeping her or what they had going on a secret. There was nothing to hide, and since she gave him the green light, Cree was smashing the gas. Yawning, Leerah stretched and eased her way off the bed. Grabbing her bonnet from underneath a pillow, she placed it over her wild hair.

"We can do that. I'ma go shower," she said.

"A'ight. Landon still with your mama?"

She nodded. "Yes. She texted me last night about them going to church and then to the water park."

"My boy be living life." Cree chuckled.

"Tell me about it."

"When you get out, we gon' run by my crib so I can get dressed."

She said okay and walked inside her bathroom, flipping the switches on. He couldn't see her from the bed but heard her when she turned the shower on. Cree lay there with not an ounce of regret. Everything felt right, down to him picking her up last night. He hoped she felt the same and truly stood on her words about being done playing games.

Five minutes into her shower, Cree slid his shorts back on. Thankfully, he had because ten minutes later, while he was using her guest bathroom, he heard knocks at the door. Not wanting to disturb her shower, Cree walked toward the door and looked through the peephole. He had no intentions of opening the door and disrespecting her crib, but he would've been even more disrespectful if he didn't answer for his godmother.

"What the hell is she doing here?" Cree questioned.

Knocking again, Andrea adjusted the Old Navy and Carter's bags in her hand. Leerah thought she was hearing things from inside the shower and brushed it off as one of her neighbors' doors. Cree twisted the locks and pulled the door open. It then hit him that he was shirtless, with no damn drawls on.

Andrea stared, tongue-tied by Cree's presence. "Oh. Hey, Cree. I, um. I wasn't expecting you to answer the door."

Cree cleared his throat. "What's up, godmama? Come in."

She stepped inside, walking fully into the open layout of the apartment. She eyed the table with remnants of a good night, spotting Cree's briefs near the couch.

"Where's Leerah?" Andrea asked, unable to hear the shower running.

"She's in the shower. Let me go put a shirt on right quick."

She waved him off, placing the bags on the

dining table. "You're fine. It seems like I'm intruding."

"You're good," Cree said, though he felt the complete opposite.

"Mhm. So, you and Leerah, huh?"

She didn't hold her tongue. Andrea heard the murmurs about them hooking up, but she wasn't feeding into the he say, she say. Had she not been in the neighborhood and dropped clothes off for Landon, she wouldn't have found out the truth this soon. She called Leerah's phone, but it was somewhere lost between her sheets. That's how she knew the dick was good; she didn't even search for it before going to shower.

"Yeah," Cree mumbled, and she glanced his way. He spoke up. "Yes."

"I'm not mad at it," she divulged, shocking him. "I'd rather it be you then anyone else."

He was humbled by her... dare he say approval. Cree wasn't for sure that's what she was giving, but Andrea made it clear with her next words.

"I say that because I know you. You're a good man, and not only does Leerah need that in her life, but Landon as well. All I want to know is if y'all were fooling around when Terrance was alive?"

"No. Never." Cree's answer was firm and the truth.

Andrea nodded. "Okay, then. And this isn't just something for y'all to do? I know how y'all young folks are. Just be fucking on anything, unwilling to settle down."

Chuckling, Cree shook his head. "Nah. It's nothing like that. I wouldn't even put her in that type of position."

"Good. Don't put yourself in that position, either. She wasn't the only person who lost someone; you did too. Make sure she handles you with the same respect you have for her."

Cree nodded. "Yes, ma'am. I hear you. We're on the same page. I wouldn't have pursued anything with her if either of us had less to give."

Andrea smiled. "And that's why I love you. Thank you for my flowers and purse, too. I can wear it on my trip coming up."

"I love you, too. Where you taking a trip to?" Cree questioned.

"Out of the country. I need a vacation."

He knew the feeling. Grief was scary and unpredictable. Sometimes, you just needed to get away. Terrance was Andrea's only child, and losing him so unexpectedly, though any way would've hurt, had almost made her lose herself. She was taking it one day at a time and taking the healing journey as it came. She prayed Leerah was doing the same.

Now out of the shower, Leerah wrapped a towel around her and stepped out of the bathroom. "Cree," she called out.

Andrea's head swiveled in the direction of her voice.

"I'm in the living room. Andrea—"

Before he could warn her about their guest, Leerah entered the living room. Her body locked up like a bad transmission seeing her standing there. She gasped so loud that Andrea couldn't help but chuckle.

"Oh, my gosh. Mrs. Andrea. I did not know you were here. I'll be right back," Leerah rushed out to say.

She walked swiftly back inside her bedroom, damn near having a panic attack. Though she didn't care for people to find out about them, Andrea, being one of the first people, was not on her agenda for today.

"She's not coming back out here, watch," Andrea said.

"She might. Let's see."

A minute later, after sliding on some leggings and a t-shirt and removing her bonnet, Leerah reappeared. Nervously, she placed distance between herself and Cree but scowled his way. *This man don' opened my door, and shirtless at that,* she said to herself.

"Hey," Leerah said, giving Andrea a hug. "How are you?"

Andrea smiled, noticing that glow in her eyes and on her face. "I'm good today. I forgot I bought this stuff for my baby and came to drop it off."

"Thank you. He's with my mama right now."

"I know. She called me yesterday. I'ma have to catch her up to speed once I get in the car, honey." She snickered.

Cree smirked, but Leerah didn't.

"She knows about us," she said.

"And now, I know about y'all, too. Sorry for intruding."

Leerah gulped. "It's fine. It's not like you don't pop up over here anyway. We just have an extra guest today." She looked at Cree.

"She's known me longer than she's known you," he said.

"Okay?" Leerah laughed. "I have a pack of cookies in the fridge since you want one so bad."

Laughing, Cree snatched her to him, ruffling her hair. "I do. Go bake me some."

Andrea looked on, smiling at their banter and closeness. She believed Cree when he said they hadn't messed with one another behind Terrance's back, but to anyone else, it wouldn't look believable. It hadn't looked believable. Leerah simmered, noticing her gaze. Rubbing her neck, she tried removing herself from his grasp, but Cree didn't let her.

"It's good seeing y'all smile," she acknowledged. "Don't let anyone take that away from y'all."

Leerah nodded, emotions heightening. "Okay. So, you don't have anything to say about this?"

"What is there to say? Cree told me there was nothing going on between y'all while Terrance was alive, and I believe him. Is that not the truth?"

"It is," Leerah stated. "I was faithful to him."

"I know you were." Andrea smiled.

She'd heard Terrance get cursed out one too many times with Leerah telling him the same exact words. *I was faithful to you!* She'd shout through the phone while looking at his mama for some type of help. After so many lectures telling him how good of a woman Leerah was, Andrea had no more advice to give.

"I'ma head on out," Andrea said. Cree walked toward the door to open it.

"Okay. Thank you for these clothes again. I'ma let him go through them when he gets home," Leerah said as they hugged goodbye.

Cree hugged her next, squeezing her frame. He kissed her forehead. "Love you, Ma. Send me the details for your trip. I'll have a lil' something for you."

Andrea did a little dance. "I know that's right, godson. Hook me up." She chuckled. "Love you, too. See y'all later."

Leerah waved, and Cree shut the door. Exhaling, he turned around. She had a look on her face that he didn't like—one that read that she was having second thoughts about them.

"You enjoy your shower?" Cree asked, trying to avoid the obvious. "I should've hopped in with you."

She shook her head no. "Cree."

"Nope. You're about to tell me some BS, and I'm not hearing it."

"It's not bullshit. Did you see how she was looking at us? Like we're some snakes," Leerah fussed.

He wasn't looking at Andrea watching them

because his eyes were too busy watching Leerah… like always. He didn't tell her that, though.

"And you heard what she said. What is there to say?"

"It's a lot to say!" Leerah yelled out of frustration.

Cree walked over to her. "Aye, listen to me. I know you're upset, but what you're not going to do is yell at me. We don't communicate like that. Lower your voice and talk to me like you want me to listen."

Leerah's chest heaved as she inhaled stuttered breaths. The dominance in his voice and words made her forget why she was yelling in the first place. He checked her without aggression and with so much respect she wanted to cry.

"I'm sorry. I'm just… afraid. This isn't wrong?"

"You've asked me that, and my answer is still no," Cree said.

Leerah pressed her hands against the sides of her face. "You're his godbrother, Cree."

"That's nothing new. I know this. We know this. Who are you?"

"The mother of his child," Leerah answered, and he shook his head.

"No. Who are *you* to *me*?" he questioned.

Leerah's eyes misted.

"Tell me," he urged.

"Your princess."

"And what do princesses get?" he asked.

She wiped the tear on her face. "Anything they want."

"Exactly. So, if you want me, I'm yours. Fuck what anyone else thinks."

Leerah wanted to scream. She wanted to say fuck everyone else, and she had been, but today... seeing Andrea had her reneging on everything she'd said.

"This is wrong," she repeated, shaking her head. "Why me? You're okay with knowing you shared me with him?"

Cree frowned. "Shared you? See, you talking crazy. If anything, I did him a solid and let him have you because you friend-zoned me after that night in your apartment."

"You had a girlfriend," Leerah cried. "If you didn't want me to be with him, you should've said that. Instead, you put him on me," she said, bending her fingers like she was quoting the words.

"Because you didn't want me." Cree scoffed. "Isn't that what you said?"

"Yes. I did say that, but it wasn't how I felt. I didn't want to get hurt."

Cree blew out a deep breath. "I would've never hurt you."

"I know that now." Leerah sniffled. "Why didn't you say anything?"

"You let it be known you only wanted to be friends, so I respected your wishes. We never crossed any lines after that night, so what else was there to say? We were friends. When I invited you out to the day party that day, Terrance was on you immediately, asking me a million questions about you. I didn't trip because I knew what it was between us. Something that happened once and nothing else."

"When y'all started messing around, he made it seem like it was nothing serious, and you were hush-hush about everything, so I didn't take it seriously. There was no need to bring up something that happened in the past. When you popped up pregnant, that's when I knew it was something more," Cree explained.

"But it wasn't even then. We weren't good for one another. I just happened to get pregnant," Leerah said.

"And that's when I knew things between us would remain the same and change. You were pregnant, Leerah," he stated, and her eyes watered more at not being called her nickname. "That's not something to play about. What did you expect me to do?"

"Still be my friend," she mumbled, sniffling.

"You're breaking my heart with these tears. Come here," he voiced, pulling her into his bare chest.

Leerah hugged him around the waist.

"I'm just so confused," she admitted.

"I know you are."

Cree rubbed her back while she got her emotions together. They'd gone from one extreme to the next in less than twenty-four hours. Arguing with her made his head hurt because it never needed to come to that. Leerah could have anything she wanted, and she knew it. Yet, the one thing he was trying to give her, she was afraid of. There was a list of things Cree wanted her to have besides his heart.

Commitment.

Support.

Attention.

Effort.

Time.

Honesty.

Protection.

Respect.

But most of all, a friendship — one where she wasn't afraid to cross the line. He thought she had gotten over it without letting others' opinions sway her love for him, but today proved she still needed more time.

Holding her at arm's length, Cree cleared his throat. "Your emotions are high right now. I understand that you feel what we are doing is wrong, and it's because everything feels right. It is right. I'm a grown man, and I've never let anyone think or make decisions for me. I want you. You hear me? That's it. If you can stand here and look me in the eyes and tell me you want and feel something different, something less than imperishable between us, then I'll let you be."

Screams of frustration bubbled at the back of her throat. Leerah wasn't confident in her answer right now. Confliction tore at her heart, and she didn't want to say the wrong thing, ultimately ruining what they had for good.

Sniffling, she asked, "You remember what I said about the water?"

Cree nodded.

"Can we... go back to testing them?"

"No."

Her eyes stretched at the finality in his voice.

"We're not going back to testing anything. I don' dove head fucking first in the water and you trying to leave me out here by myself."

"But I'm—"

Cree cut her off with a kiss on the lips. "Find you a life jacket and come get me. I'll be here waiting for you."

With that, he walked back into her bedroom to retrieve his phone and belongings. Leerah wanted to say much more. He left her with a lot to think about but if she didn't hurry and make up her mind, Cree was going to drown and there'd be no saving him, then. There'd be no saving either of them, and that's what she didn't want to happen.

"JUST SORTING THROUGH MY FEELINGS NOW."

TEN

"Leerah, I don't know what you want me to tell you that I already haven't," Sovanna said into the phone.

"Tell me it again. I'm sad." Leerah pouted.

Sovanna chuckled. "That man wants to be with you. I see it. You see it. Everyone sees it, but you. Maybe you need to make an appointment at Vision-works. It's one near you."

"Shut up! I can see just fine. I'm just scared. What if I lose him, too?"

An overflow of sadness washed over Sovanna. "Awww, friend. You won't. Don't think like that."

"But I could," Leerah countered. "I have before. He really stopped fooling with me when I started messing with Terrance."

"What did you expect him to do? Some men do have morals," Sovanna said.

Leerah sucked her teeth as she pushed her car through traffic. "They do. I wasn't expecting us to mess around. I wasn't on that, and we both made that clear, but he acted like he was scared to speak to me or something."

She hated how they'd gone from the best of friends to almost strangers. Leerah didn't even feel comfortable in the same spaces as Cree. His energy was so off-putting, and Leerah caught herself catching an attitude with him for no reason. She was the one to blame for their distance—the distance that she requested as Cree's friend.

She finally confessed and told Sovanna what happened between her and Cree in college. It had been so far removed from her mind that she didn't think it needed to be shared, especially since they had agreed to keep things platonic.

"The man was trying to remain loyal. Have you seen you?" Sovanna asked.

Leerah smirked. "I'm some pressure, huh?"

"Big pressure, friend. That man would've folded quicker than a lawn chair, and you know it."

"Yeah, well, he didn't, and now we're here. And I miss him so much," Leerah whined.

It'd been a week since she'd been so-called searching for a life jacket, and so far, she'd come up emptyhanded. Cree was still holding on, though. *He could've played Jack for real,* Leerah thought and chuckled.

"He must've put it on you *real* bad." Sovanna giggled.

"Listen. When he dropped his shorts and that dick popped out, my heart didn't skip a beat; my coochie did. Then, she flatlined."

Sovanna laughed so loud on the other end of the phone, Leerah had to turn the volume in her car down.

"You truly have no sense!" She wheezed, wiping her eyes. "Grow up."

"My time is coming. Everyone can't be like you and meet your man in the club after letting him slut you out."

Sovanna snickered. "Yeah, yeah. You could've."

"Mhm," Leerah hummed. "I did grow up some. Just sorting through my feelings now. I'm headed to see Terrance."

"Is Landon with you?"

"No. I'm going alone today," Leerah answered. "Got him some new flowers to put down."

"I'm sure he'll like that."

Leerah nodded. "Probably not from me, but oh well. I'm pulling in here now, though, so I'll call you when I leave."

"Okay. I'm at home, the one my job pays for, so you can come over if you want to."

"Okay. I'll call and let you know."

They hung up, and Leerah pulled slowly onto the side of the paved lane. She parked underneath a tree, trying to keep her car as shaded as possible. It was so hot out and the wind was nowhere in sight. A slight breeze would've been perfect. Taking a few deep breaths, Leerah gazed out the window. She wanted to enjoy a few more minutes of the air.

Grabbing the bags from Dollar General, she climbed out of her car and left it running. Memory helped her navigate through the tombstones until she approached his. It'd been months since she visited. Leerah hadn't quite come to terms with the way she had to see him now. It hurt, but it hurt more when she brought Landon. Today, the grief didn't feel as heavy. Her guilt did.

"I know you're probably saying, what am I doing here with my scandalous ass." She chuckled, pulling the tags off the fake flowers.

"Well, I need to get some things off my chest, and you're going to listen," she said, removing the old flowers and replacing them with vibrant royal blue and white ones.

"First of all, your son has gotten so big, and he looks just like you. Every time he smiles or does little expressions, I just be like, damn, you are your daddy's child." She chuckled, feeling an onset of tears pool in her eyes. "We miss you so much. Nothing has felt the same since you've been gone, but nothing has really changed, either. Except for your presence. Every bill is paid, nothing is behind, our families are still supportive, and Misha is still messy."

Life wasn't normal anymore, but it hadn't crippled her like it'd done in the first few weeks of him being gone. Leerah had to learn to shake back quickly for her son, and her community was a big reason why she could.

"And guess who I ran into? Mhm. Little Ms. Ashley. You got that hoe pregnant, Terrance? Really? I'll give it to her, she's cute, but I can't believe you slid up in her raw. That's so crazy."

Leerah felt so comfortable talking to him. Whatever she felt she needed to say just came naturally, as if he could hear her and respond. Using a Clorox wipe, she wiped off his headstone, making it reveal its glossiness.

"Oh, and I'm sure your mama told you, but I almost beat your auntie's ass. That's all I'ma say on that."

She hadn't found another daycare yet, and Andrea was trying to convince her to let Landon stay at Little Learners. If they fired Vee, that's where he'd be. Until then, Landon was staying with her oldest brother's wife during the week. She was a stay-at-home mom of one and didn't mind Landon coming over at all. Leerah knew that wouldn't last for long, though. Plus, she didn't want to feel like a burden and overuse their welcome. Removing the blanket from the bag, she unfolded it and sat down.

"I had to get comfortable for this next conversation," she said and tilted her head back toward the sky before dropping it back down. "I'm seeing, Cree. It's probably something I should've told you way before now, but I didn't. It didn't happen overnight, and maybe it was disloyal of me to not tell you we were intimate, but I didn't see the point. Boundaries had been established between us by the time you and I met."

Leerah huffed and grabbed a bottle of water. Twisting the cap, she chugged half of it down. "Got me out here explaining myself in this fucking heat. You better have done this for me if the roles were reversed," she fussed, then giggled. "I know you would've."

A thought so loud entered her brain. *Would Cree?* Leerah frowned. The words sounded so clear, but she couldn't make out whose voice they were spoken in.

"Cree definitely would have," she said aloud.

Her eyes focused on the custom-made heart-shaped wind chime she placed in the ground some months back. It had an engraved note from her to Terrance on it.

"I know I sound crazy, but can you send me a sign? Something to let me know that you won't haunt me for messing around with him. I want to move on and be happy. Not forget you, because that will never happen, but just be happy, Terrance. Cree makes me happy," she said, deeply inhaling. "And he loves Landon so much. You'd want that, right? Someone to truly take care of not just him but me, too."

She closed her eyes, waiting to see if she heard anything or felt his presence. Leerah wasn't sure what to wait for, but her heart lurched, and her eyes shot open when the tubes on the wind chime began to move.

"Oh, my gosh," she whispered.

Her head swiveled to stare at the trees. None of them were moving. The tubes continued to create a harmonious, tinkling sound that brought tears to her eyes.

"Wow. Thank you for not being stubborn today." She chuckled. Kissing her index and middle finger, she placed it against his headstone. "Rest peacefully, baby daddy."

After gathering her trash, Leerah got back in her car and sat there for a few minutes. Receiving a sign from Terrance had blown her mind, but it also confirmed what she needed to do. It was time to let go her fear of being loved.

You don't only grieve people when they pass away, but things, too. Memories that were created together, restaurants you no longer eat at because it was with them, a certain scent they wore that you try to avoid, and even songs that come on and make you think of them. Those were the small things. Grief was an aggressive bitch, but Leerah was ready to fight back.

She was grieving the hold fear had on her, burying it in an empty spot in the grass. Fear had no place in her life if she wanted to move forward and truly give herself and Cree a chance.

"I'm in town until next week. Hopefully, you'll make time for me." Veronica, Cree's mama, said over the phone.

Cree stared blankly at the seconds on the phone as time passed. He hadn't been expecting her call. They were few and far between, but it was good to hear her voice. He was surprised she was stopping through to show her face for more than a day or two.

"Yeah, I can do that. Where you staying at?" Cree questioned.

"We got a room at Loews."

She and her husband, DeAngelo, a millionaire baseball player from Seattle. Cree had met him once... or was it twice? He couldn't recall. Her son's opinion of him didn't matter to Veronica. Not completely. *As long as she's happy,* Cree thought.

"That's cool. Where you at right now?"

"At The Legend's. As if I need anything else to fill my closet." She chuckled. The outlet mall should've been far off her radar, but she couldn't help herself.

Cree smirked. "Right. You want to go out to dinner tomorrow?"

"I'd love that, baby. I'd say today, but Andrea and I are meeting up later. I have to get my girl out of the house. Did she tell you we were going to Greece next month?" Veronica asked.

So, that was her trip out of the country, he thought. "No, she didn't tell me that. Greece is a well-deserved vacation spot."

"It certainly is. All paid, too. I can't imagine what she's been going through, and my quick turnaround trips to visit her haven't been enough."

Cree sat up some in his chair. "What you mean quick turnaround trips? You been in the city?"

Veronica chuckled. "Of course, I have. You know I was traveling back and forth when Terrance first passed. Now it's once or twice a month if work allows."

"I didn't know that," Cree said, feeling a way.

"I don't have to always tell you when I'm in town, Cree." She giggled. "My best friend needed me, so I was there. You show up for the people you love when they need you."

He drew his head back, finding her words funny. "I'm glad you figured that whole showing up thing out. Modeling gigs must be slowing up."

Veronica stopped shuffling through the racks inside Banana Republic. "Did I say something wrong?"

The softness and confusion in her voice made Cree want to take his words back. Not because he didn't mean them but because of how she made him feel after saying them. Regardless of how she so subtly abandoned him, leaving the duty of raising him to his grandparents, Cree's heart was still soft towards her.

"No. You're good, Ma," he said, standing from his seat. "Finish shopping and hit me up later."

Veronica hesitated, detecting the frustration in his tone, but she didn't press the issue. She never did. She let things be what they were going to be. "Um, okay. I'll call you later, then. Love you."

"Love you, too," Cree replied and tapped the red circle to end the call.

Exhaling, he looked around his office at nothing in particular. He just needed to stand up. Her words jarred him, and as much as Cree wanted to understand her decisions as a mother, he couldn't. He wouldn't. There was no use in dwelling over them. Despite her shortcomings in their relationship, he had no less love for her. But that was also why he fell hard for Leerah. The way she cared for Landon during the midst of her grief was admirable and made Cree want to take the weight off her. It was okay to not be strong all the time, and he hoped she knew that.

A knock at his door grabbed his attention. "Knock, knock. I have a special delivery for you," Persia, his assistant, said.

Cree glanced down at the container of cookies in her hand. A card with his name scribbled on top was taped to the clear covering.

"You got these?" he asked.

"Nope. Someone dropped them off and asked that they be given to you."

Taking the container out of her hand, Cree sat it on the console against the wall. "That's love. Appreciate you for bringing them back."

"Mhm. No problem. Hopefully, they cheer you up," Persia hinted.

Cree chuckled. "I been looking sad or something?"

"A little bit, but everyone has their days. Just don't let the days make you. Everything will be just fine," she said, dropping gems. Persia made it to the door but then quickly spun around. "Don't forget about the meeting with Boss and Saleem in an hour."

His head bobbed once. "I won't. I'm sure your reminder will pop up in forty-five minutes."

Persia chuckled. "I'm glad you know."

She walked out, leaving Cree with a screw face. He hadn't felt like himself all week, but he didn't know other people could tell. Only one person was the cause of his moping, but she wouldn't be for long.

Removing the envelope from the lid, Cree grabbed the card out. His laugh bounced off the walls at the image on the front. Only Leerah could buy him a card with a swimmer on it and a message that let him know she was ready for everything he had to offer. The homemade cookies from one of her homegirl's bakeries were the true peace offering.

If you dare to dip your toe into the vast, rushing currents of life, you may discover that all you truly ever wanted to do was swim.

Cree read the words twice, letting them marinate. Leerah was telling him that she was ready to take that dive. He knew she would be.

Unlike before, Cree's texts didn't get ignored nor did his phone calls. They just never brought up the elephant in the room. Like he promised to be, Cree was patient and still here when she was ready.

Flipping the card open, he smirked and read it aloud. "Let's go swimming. Please bring a damn floatie."

He cracked up at her personal note before placing it back inside the envelope. Before pulling his phone out to call her, he grabbed one of the cookies. He counted a dozen, and with the way they tasted, he'd be demolishing all twelve and working it off later in the week. Cree closed the door to his office as he waited for her to answer his FaceTime call. She was off work today, so he knew she was at home. When the call connected, Cree was looking at her ceiling.

"Don't call me smacking on those cookies," she said, making him chuckle.

"Dang, Princess. Hello, to you, too."

She picked the phone up so he could see her. "Hi." She smiled.

"You got you a moo-moo on." Cree chuckled. "You chilling, huh?"

"I sure am."

She loved her a comfortable sleep dress from

Wal-Mart, especially if it had pockets. Leerah would throw one on quickly after a shower. Cree just stared at the screen, admiring her. Her hair was in chunky twists, drying so that she could wear a twist-out. With the way her hair was set up, Leerah was going to need all day for it to dry to her likeness. Her answering the phone with no reservations as to how she may have looked was why Cree loved her.

Damn. I'm in love with this woman, he thought and cleared his throat.

"That's what's up. What you over there doing?" He heard the music in the background but wanted to see what she had going on.

Leerah flipped the camera around, panning it over her lap and the couch. Her crochet hook sat in the dip of her shirt while a basket of colorful yarn was by her feet.

"You know… the usual. I'm off today, so I'm just enjoying some time to myself," she said.

"Yeah, I see that. You took the time out of your day to send me a special delivery, too. I appreciate that, baby. Thank you."

Leerah grinned. "You're welcome. You like the card?" She chuckled.

"Yeah. That's your way of letting me know you're ready for this?"

She nodded. "I am. You told me to come find you, so I sent a bat signal with some food. Well, cookies."

"Do the cookies come with you? I'd rather be eating you instead," Cree said, and Leerah almost dropped the phone.

Smirking, she said, "I mean, they can. It's nothing to come see you. You gon' bend me over your desk?"

"I will, but I'd prefer sliding up in you while you on a balcony with an ocean view. How that sound?" Cree asked.

Leerah tossed the throw blanket off her legs. He had her hot and bothered. "Like we need to book a trip ASAP. When can you take off work?"

Cree chuckled. "I'm the boss, Princess. This place will run while I'm gone and enjoying you. Look up some places and tell me how much you need."

"Just like that, huh?"

"That's exactly how it's gon' be. Forever," Cree stated and winked. "Can you do me a favor, though?"

Leerah brushed an eyelash off her cheek. "Mhm. What?"

"Make sure Lando has a babysitter tomorrow. I'm taking you out."

Her face lit up. "Where?"

"You'll find out tomorrow."

She squinted her eyes and smirked. "Okay. I'ma trust you."

"That's all I ever need you to do. So, about you bending over my desk. I just cleared it off. Come see me."

Leerah rubbed her neck. "Right now?"

"Yeah, don't be shy now. We can go get lunch. Wait, I have a meeting in a minute. I'll just come by when I get off."

"Okay."

"Lando at daycare?" he asked.

She nodded. "Yes. I kept him in there. They moved Vee to another grade level, so I was okay with that."

"Good. Want me to pick him up so you don't have to leave the house?"

Leerah simpered and nodded. It was always the simple things that Cree did that made her love for him expand beyond what she ever thought it could. *Yeah, I love this fine ass man,* she thought, then answered his question.

"Yes, you can. Thank you."

Cree smirked. "You're welcome. I'm proud of you. Just a few months ago, you would've told me you didn't need me to do anything for you."

She rolled her eyes. "Yeah, well, I've grown. So, thank you. I'm learning that it's okay to let you be here for me."

Cree's heart swelled inside his chest. Hearing those words seemingly made all things right in the world. Leerah hadn't realized it until after she visited Terrance's grave, but she was surrounded by angels—Cree being the main one. God had sent him to her when Leerah needed him the most. It made her feel like He hadn't forgotten about her after all, and He never would.

"YOU GOT ME, PRINCESS."

ELEVEN

Weeks Later

Cree walked inside Leerah's bedroom with his phone glued to his ear. He was there more days out of the week than at his crib. Leerah didn't mind it, and Landon didn't either. His presence was welcomed.

"It's the week of a holiday, so more security has to be present," Cree said, speaking to one of his newest property managers. "Yeah. You know how folks get. It's all good. We're not open on Thursday, but open up bright and early at eight, Friday morning."

He conversed for a few more minutes, ensuring everything was squared away before hanging up. Though he owned the shopping center and wasn't as present during the day-to-day operations, his line was still open if they needed guidance. Cree knew that with the Fourth of July a few days away, he'd be getting a few more phone calls. People seemed to lose their minds when any holiday approached.

Standing in front of her floor-length mirror with her panties and a cami tank top on, Leerah admired her body. As discussed, she and the girls started their fitness journey last month, and Leerah couldn't believe the subtle changes she was already seeing. Nae told her not to focus on the scale so much but on how she felt and how her clothes fit. So far, Leerah felt like she had so much more energy and some of her pants and shirts fit looser. Cree stepped behind her and lovingly caressed her booty before smacking it.

He kissed her cheek and said, "You looking good, baby."

Blushing, Leerah fastened her eyes on him through the mirror. "Thank you. You have a good nap?"

Cree yawned, wrapping a hand around her waist, nestling his face in the crook of her neck. "Mhm. Until Benny called. It's all good, though. I needed to get up anyway. We got about an hour before we need to head out."

"What time are the reservations?" Leerah asked and shivered as he kissed her neck.

"Seven," Cree answered, rubbing her body down.

Large hands massaged her thighs and trailed up her belly before disappearing underneath her tank top. Cree balanced her large breasts in his hands, squeezing them gently. A breathy moan fell from Leerah's lips when his thumbs lightly brushed over her nipples. She gasped when he pinched them, rolling them between his fingers.

"Sss, mmm," she moaned, letting her head fall back against his chest.

Cree toyed with the one he learned was most sensitive while his other hand ventured between her legs smoothly. Ovulation week had Leerah a sticky, dripping, horny mess. His fingers rubbed the seat of her panties, making her clit swell. She stroked his dick through his briefs before sticking her hand inside. He was so warm in her palm that Leerah wanted to feel him in her mouth.

"Don't start something you can't finish," Cree said.

Leerah lifted her head and smirked, watching them in the mirror. "You started with me."

He rubbed firmer against the wet cotton. Leerah

stepped away and turned to face him when she felt herself about to come.

"Lay down," she insisted.

Licking his lips, Cree smirked and began walking backward to her bed, but she grabbed his hand.

"Right here," Leerah said, directing him to the plush cream rug in front of the mirror.

Doing as told, Cree lowered his briefs and laid on his back. His dick pierced the air like a tower, long and thick, ready to please her. Being courteous, Leerah grabbed one of the feather pillows from the bed and placed it behind his head. Stripping from panties, she twisted her lips, trying to decide her next move.

"This a lot of dick you about to ride," Cree warned, stroking himself.

Leerah grinned. "Mhm. I know. How do you want me?"

"It doesn't even matter. Come hop on this motha-fucka, Princess."

Cree didn't often curse unless he was in that mood or had been drinking, and Leerah loved it. Something about him telling her to sit on his pole with that grit of an accent in his tone made her pussy wetter. Facing away from him, she lowered into a squat, positioning her legs underneath his thighs. Cree's arm stretched out to rub her ass as her wetness engulfed him.

"Oooh, fuck," Leerah moaned.

"Damn," Cree muttered in pure pleasure.

She glided on him with ease and rolled her hips. Penetration from this angle was going to make her come so quickly, and she could feel the build-up already.

"You hear that pussy talking to me?" Cree asked, spanking her ass.

"Mhm."

Cree kept his eyes on their connection until Leerah looked back at him. Her bottom lip was tucked between her teeth, and her walls gripped him so tightly that Cree's toes cracked. He thrust his hips, making Leerah gush. Climbing to her feet with him still inside, Leerah positioned them on the outside of his thighs, gripped his knees, and began to bounce.

Smack! Smack!

"Look at you," Cree groaned. "Riding my dick like this."

Leerah's entire body trembled. "Oh my gosh," she cried.

Her moans were loud, matching the sounds of their lovemaking. It didn't matter that they'd just gotten it in hours earlier while Landon took a nap before getting dropped off at Leerah's brother's house. Their appetite for one another was insatiable. Gripping an ass cheek, she rode him with fervor, riding the waves of pleasure.

"Mmh. That's a good girl, Princess. Fuck me just like that."

Cree's encouragement made her go harder, shaking as she kept coming. A moan stalled in her throat when he sat up, propping his feet up. Gripping her waist, Cree pounded into her.

"Fuuuuck!" Leerah whimpered on the verge of tears.

Cree held her tighter. "I know, I know. Let that nut go, Princess. Let me feel it."

She climaxed hard, wetting him and the rug beneath them up. Not letting up, Cree stroked her until he felt his nut approached. She felt it, too. Climbing off him, Leerah positioned herself between his legs. Seeing his glistening pole made her mouth water and eyes sparkle with unfiltered lust.

"Tell me how good you taste," Cree said, ready to feel her mouth.

There was something so profound about taking on a challenge and exceeding what was expected of her. Cree's dick was big; there was no other way to say it. But, Leerah had grown accustomed to receiving him. It'd penetrated her walls in a way that would never leave her with a sane thought whenever he was on her mind. She wanted to leave him with the same certifiable ideas while taking him down her throat. In her mind, it was only right.

"Sss. Damn," Cree hissed as he held her head in place.

His dick elongated down her throat. Leerah kept her mouth wide as he pumped his hips, making her gag. Controlled breaths released through her nostrils as she stared at him.

"Don't look at me like that," Cree groaned, pleading while squeezing his eyes shut.

A loud slurping echoed around them as she pulled her mouth off and spit on his pole before jacking him off. "Like what?" Leerah asked, smiling.

Cree opened his eyes to reply, but the words left his brain as she swallowed him again. His hand fell from her hair, and Leerah went to work. Back and forth, her head bobbed, wanting to pull that nut right up out of him. They were pressed for time, but some quick head never hurt anyone.

The way her lips stretched around him, swollen and wet, Cree's nut crept up on him quicker than he thought. He was sure it hadn't been a full six minutes yet. Leerah hummed, enjoying the taste of him.

"You so pretty sucking my dick. Com'ere," Cree slurred. She had him feeling drunk.

Leerah popped him out of her mouth, and she was snatched to Cree's mouth by her jaw. He was gentle with it but tongued her down roughly. A hand slipped between her legs as they kissed. She was so wet and turned on but knew they'd really be late if they went another round.

"Mmm. We have to hurry up," she said, pulling away and placing her mouth right back on his length.

It was so pretty; Leerah only sucked on the tip so she could admire it and her handy work. She twirled her tongue around him, twisting and stroking him with one hand that she couldn't get completely around him.

"Yeah...mhmm. Keep sucking it just like that," Cree coached.

Like the star player she was, Leerah followed instructions and didn't ease up until his creamy thickness spurt out on her stretched tongue. Some dripped down her chin, but she swallowed and licked up most of it. Cree's body trembled as she slurped on the tip, popping him out of her mouth after a job well done.

"Nice little protein shot for the win." She giggled, standing to her feet.

Cree's eyes fluttered as he wrapped an arm around her waist. "I love you."

A surge of happiness washed over her, simmering the lust in her eyes. Cree's declaration was unexpected but very much so appreciated. Leerah didn't know how much of a relief she felt hearing those words. He'd reassured her in the best way possible, letting it be known that what she felt for him was reciprocated. Everything she'd told him and he'd witnessed had been valued.

"Awww," she cooed, wrapping her arms around him. "I love you, too."

"You mean that?" Cree asked, brushing a spiral of hair out of her face.

She nodded. "I mean that shit with my whole heart, Cree. And I know you mean it, too."

"How you figure that?" he asked in jest, smirking.

"Because, silly. I just sucked you thoughtless. There's no way you would've professed that without a clear mind." She kissed his soft lips again. "I mean, probably, but this moment was perfect. You should thank me for making you come to that realization."

Cree laughed. "I came to it before now, but thank you *so* much, Princess Leerah. How gracious of you to make me come to my senses."

She giggled. "Literally. Shout out to me. Now, let's get dressed. I'm hungry and ready to eat."

"You didn't just eat enough?" Cree asked and laughed as she slapped his arm.

"Boy, quit playing with me, and come on!"

She turned out of his grasp and walked toward the bathroom.

Reaching out, Cree smacked her booty and grinned. "Yes, ma'am. I'm right behind you."

EVERMORE
SERIES

Besides her parents' wedding, Leerah hadn't attended many in her life. There'd been a few here and there of friends from college, but that was it. It didn't make her believe less in love; it made her want to experience it for herself one day.

Truthfully, it wasn't even about marriage. It was more about sharing an unbreakable, life-altering, soul-bending, heart-stirring love—the kind that molds you into a greater human being. That's what

Leerah wanted, and watching the newlywed couple share their first dance had her wondering what hers would be like after making it down the aisle.

"They look so in love," she gushed as Cree walked back to their table.

He sat their drinks down and glanced her way. He'd been staring all evening and couldn't wait to get her home. He made sure she could be his plus-one to a business friend's wedding.

"That's how you gon' look," Cree said and casually sipped from his drink.

Leerah smirked. "Is that right?"

"Yeah. What, you don't think I'd change your last name?"

"I know you will," she breathed, licking her lips.

He nodded. "Glad we're on the same page. Here, taste this," he said, extending his straw to her glossy lips.

Her eyes brightened. "Ooh. That's good. What is that?"

"Some type of mango wine and D'Ussé mix."

"You know what they say about D'Ussé." Leerah chuckled, picking up her cup.

Cree cut his mesmerizing eyes at her. "Nah. What they be saying?"

"It'll make you do whatever I say."

"I don't even need a drink for that." Cree laughed. "You got me, Princess. I promise you that."

Leerah puckered her lips out for a kiss. Obliging, Cree pressed his against hers. This wasn't their first outing together since they made things official months ago, but it was one she'd remembered forever. They'd known each other for years, but there were people in their lives that neither had met. Cree had introduced her to people that made her want to continue bossing her life up.

There wasn't anything wrong with the job she had as a radiology technologist, but being around entrepreneurs who created their own schedules and lived more flexible lives, had her reconsidering. For now, though, she was happy. It'd taken a while to get there and mean it, but the trials had been worth it.

When the couple of the hour made their way around the room, Cree stood and helped her to her feet. Leerah smiled, loving the bride's custom MAG Co. dress. As soon as she saw the gorgeous pearl and diamond material, with sheer corset detailing in the back, Leerah had to do some research. According to one of the women sitting beside her, a local Black-owned clothing brand had designed it.

"Congratulations, my boy," Cree said, dapping

and giving the groom a brotherly hug. "You clean, ain't you."

Synovi smirked and nodded his head in Leerah's direction. "Thank you, thank you. This all my Love's doing."

Stunning as ever, Torin smiled. "I can't take all the credit."

"When I say you are killing that dress, honey. Yes, ma'am. Congratulations to you both," Leerah told her.

"Thank you so much!" Torin beamed and then addressed Cree. "Novi has mentioned your name to me, reminding me to partner with you at the strip mall, but I keep forgetting. It's good to finally put a face with your name."

Humbly, Cree nodded. "Likewise. All we hear at the gym is Love this, Love that," he said, making them laugh. "I must say, love does look good on y'all."

Smiling brightly, Torin leaned into her husband's side, and his hand circled her snatched waist. "Thank you. It does on y'all, too."

Cree glanced Leerah's way, and she blushed. He had to agree with Torin. They walked off to greet more guests and the couple reclaimed their seats. Leerah people watched, giggling at a few of the folks who had indulged a bit too much at the open bar already.

"I tell you how fine you look tonight?" Cree whispered in her ear.

She placed a hand on his thigh. "Mhm, but you can tell me again."

"I can tell you all night, and my words still wouldn't suffice."

Leerah kissed his cheek as he drank from his straw. She had to admit, they did look good as hell tonight. Cree's cream-colored suit and burgundy shirt, with a few buttons undone at the top, looked so good against his dark skin. His fade was fresh, and Leerah had been sniffing his neck all night because he smelled heavenly.

He matched her fly as she had on a burgundy silk midi-dress that came to her knees and had a scoop neck. She paired it with gold accessories, styling her hair in flirty, beach wave curls. Before they left his crib, they took some pictures.

When Cree posted a few on his social media pages, both their phones started blowing up with texts and phone calls. Those who already knew about them weren't surprised, but the ones who didn't had a ton of questions that would never be answered. It was truly one of those *if you know, you know*, situations.

The DJ for the evening had the jams going and hadn't missed yet. She catered to the younger and older crowd yet still kept it respectful for the older generation in attendance. When the beat dropped to the next song, all the ladies' faces lit up, and Cree glanced at Leerah. She was part of the bunch, using her fisted hand as a microphone, her body swaying from side to side. He chuckled, hearing her struggling vocals.

Cree noticed how into *Love All Over Me* by Monica she was, singing her heart out. He knew she wanted to get up and dance by the way she was longingly staring at him while doing so. Standing up, he adjusted his suit jacket and extended his hand. Leerah's hand flew over her mouth as she smiled widely. Knowing her man did not like to dance but was willing to for her had her in shock. Cree helped her from her seat.

"May I have this dance, Princess?" he asked.

Leerah nodded and took his hand, allowing him to lead her to the dance floor. Her arms draped over his shoulders and Cree held her protectively around the waist. Body to body, heart to heart, they swayed to the sultry, captivating song that was laced with lyrics meant for them. Cree grinned as she sang in his face, speaking directly to his heart.

"This your song, huh?" Cree asked.

Leerah nodded. "Yes. I can't believe I got you out here dancing. You must really love me."

"I do," he said, kissing her lips. "Thank you for giving us a chance."

Chuckling, she said, "You didn't give me a choice."

"I gave you a few. I'm just glad you made the right one. Just know I got you and Landon forever."

Months ago, Leerah would've doubted his words, but Cree had made her a believer. Now, she could confidently wrap her arms around him, knowing that his words were golden... just like his heart, and she could trust him with hers.

EPILOGUE

Months Later

Leerah sat on the phone with Sovanna, congratulating her on her new position as the permanent business development manager of Oasis Hotel. She called her on her lunch break after receiving an offer letter through email. It came with higher pay, a hefty stipend to help her settle in her new home, and some of the best benefits a woman could ask for.

"I'm so damn happy, I could cry," Leerah said.

Sovanna laughed. "You? I already cried once. And I was talking about I'm not moving back." She chuckled.

"Right. You moved back and got yourself a man and a promotion. Let me pull up my email and see if I've been blessed," Leerah said, making them laugh.

She was off work early for the day and was glad about it. Still, she was on her MacBook doing some online shopping for their trip in a few months.

"Girl, Cree is the blessing. Where is he and my baby?"

"On their way home. He's picking him up from Misha's house."

Sovanna pursed her lips out. "Okay, now. That's big."

"I know, right? Tink called and asked if he could spend the night. You know I couldn't say no."

It was a huge step for her to let Landon spend the night over at someone's house, but she was trying. It did help that Misha had a son one year older than Landon, and she hadn't been on her usual messiness. Leerah figured if she could mature some, so could she.

"That's good for y'all. Little family bonding," Sovanna teased, making Leerah playfully roll her eyes.

A knock resounded through Sovanna's office, and she told whoever it was to come in. Zahir pushed the door open, carrying roses in one hand and a bottle of champagne in the other. Sovanna's face lit up.

"Awww, bae. You didn't have to bring me flowers," Sovanna cooed.

"Let me see." Leerah grinned, happy for her friend.

She couldn't flip the camera quickly enough. Zahir was at her side, placing the case down and giving her the nastiest, proudest kiss Leerah had ever witnessed. The phone slipped from Sovanna's hand and Leerah clapped.

"Okay! I know that's right, Zahir. You better celebrate your woman."

Pulling away from him, Sovanna blushed and ran her thumb over his bottom lip. "Thank you, baby."

"You're welcome. Congratulations, baby doll," he said. "What's up, Leerah."

"Hey! Vonna, congrats again, friend. I'ma let you go but know we're going out to celebrate this weekend. Everything on me, with your boss ass!"

Sovanna smiled. "We can do that. Love you. I'll call you when I get off."

"You off right now," Zahir noted. "I'm here to pick you up."

"Oop. I heard that. I love you, too. I guess, call me when you're not—"

Sovanna disconnected the call before Leerah could start talking crazy. Laughing, Leerah placed her phone on the bed. Waking up her MacBook screen, she navigated to her emails. Her brows dipped, spotting an email that she would normally send right to the trash folder. Although she paid some of her loans down, Leerah was confused as to why Nelnet continued to send her emails.

"Those loans are called student loans. I am no longer a student, baby. Those belong to God," she said, tapping the email.

She began to hyperventilate as she read over the first few sentences. Her vision blurred when she reread it, then finally made it to the end of the email. Leerah's hands trembled as she reached for her phone to call Cree. As soon as it unlocked, she heard them come through the front door. It couldn't have been better timing because she was about to pass out.

"Mama, Mama," Landon chanted, running directly to her.

A dinosaur was in one hand, while his blue sippy cup occupied the other. Leerah couldn't even speak to him, only rub a shaky hand over his neat braids she put in earlier in the week. They were still intact because Cree bought him a du-rag. Noticing that she hadn't said anything, Cree walked over to the couch.

"Baby… what's wrong? You didn't hear Lando? Why you looking like that?" Cree asked, touching her face. He didn't know what he was looking for, but she was scaring him.

Her voice shook as she tried to formulate a sentence. "You… what did you… you paid off my student loans?"

Cree smiled like it was nothing. To him, it wasn't. "Yeah. Are those happy or sad tears?" He questioned as one slid down her cheek.

Leerah wiped it away. "Shock, confusion, happy tears. I don't know. Why would—"

Cree gave her a look that halted the question she hadn't asked in months. "Why would I what, huh?"

"Nothing," she said, shaking her head. "I just… that's crazy. I was paying on them. We haven't even been together that long for you to be making such a huge financial decision like that."

"Are you mad because I didn't tell you?" Cree asked.

"No, I'm not mad… just overwhelmed. Do you know how much money that was?"

Cree laughed. "Yeah, baby, I do. I paid it."

He paid it off without blinking. Without thought. It was nothing for him and everything for Leerah. Cree didn't know how much clearer he could get. Leerah shook her head and he continued.

"My idea of you in a committed relationship with me is one where you don't have to worry about anything I can control."

Leerah cocked her head to the side, and he already knew what she was thinking, so he clarified.

"I'm not saying I'm trying to control you. What I'm saying is as your man, I want to see you at your best. That can't happen if you're worried about bills and debt that can be handled by me... your man," he explained.

"But... thirty bands isn't just some tiny bill, Cree."

"It's not tiny to you, Princess. Money flows through my hands in abundance; if I touch it, you touching it, too. So, where you trying to go from here 'cause me and Lando hungry."

She rubbed a hand over her forehead and smiled. "I guess nowhere. You're going to take care of me however you want."

He kissed her lips. "I been telling you this. Save your money for your crotchet business you've been talking to me about. I'ma invest in that, too. You can put whatever else in Landon's college fund. Quit tripping. I got y'all."

"Forever?" Leerah asked, smiling, already knowing his answer.

"Forever."

AFTERWORD

Leerah and Cree's story was one I had to tap into. Their voices were so loud way before Heat Of The Moment was completed. What started out as a novella in my mind, became a novel on screen overnight. Cree is a good man, honey, and my girl Leerah deserved everything he had to give.

ACKNOWLEDGMENTS

All praise to the Man above for blessing me with a gift and allowing me to share it with the world. I'm forever grateful!

Thank you to every reader who supports me! If you enjoyed the book, please be sure to leave a review when you can and tell a reader friend about it.

To my cover reveal and ARC team, you don't know how much I appreciate you! Thank you for going above and beyond for me. I hope y'all are ready for the rest of the year!

DISCUSSION QUESTIONS

Would you have crossed the line with Cree or Leerah?

Was Leerah wrong for kissing him?

Should Leerah have told Terrance about their past, or was that up to Cree?

Do you think Vee got what she deserved?

Do you think Cree's intentions were pure?

Is Saleem and Amira's story up next?